To Colin

SOMEWHERE BETWEEN MYTH, MYSTERY, AND MADNESS

BY

RICHARD PARR

with best regards
Topper (Tony)

DORRANCE PUBLISHING CO., INC.
PITTSBURGH, PENNSYLVANIA 15222

The contents of this work, including, but not limited to, the accuracy of events, people, and places depicted; opinions expressed; permission to use previously published materials included; and any advice given or actions advocated are solely the responsibility of the author, who assumes all liability for said work and indemnifies the publisher against any claims stemming from publication of the work.

ISBN: 978-1-4349-0047-0
Library of Congress Control Number: 2008901093

Printed in the United States of America

First Printing

For more information or to order additional books, please contact:
Dorrance Publishing Co., Inc.
701 Smithfield Street
Third Floor
Pittsburgh, Pennsylvania 15222
U.S.A.
1-800-788-7654
www.dorrancebookstore.com

SOMEWHERE BETWEEN

MYTH...

MYSTERY...

AND MADNESS!

RICHARD PARR

In memory of my dad and Harvey.

Made possible with the patience of my wife.

Thanks to all the boys for their help and support in writing this book, particularly those that will recognize their actions against another name.

It is for the reader to decide;
What is myth?
And what is mystery?
And for those affected...
remember, madness is an aid to your sanity!

This is not 'one of those SAS books'!
This is the first part of an interesting story.

Chapter One

2001. Great year!

After all I had been through, this just takes the biscuit.

"Leave the Army; find a relaxing but challenging job. Don't think about the past, let it lie. It's gone now, its all in the past. It can't hurt you anymore."

.confused!

Why are all the police here?

Why are they carrying guns?

That smell? That familiar smell. What is it?

"You okay?" asked a 5'6" female police officer, wearing body armor that looked big enough to cover a 6'5" male.

She carried an MP5 machine pistol.

"What's going on?" I asked. My tongue felt like it had been stuck to the roof of my mouth.

Before she could answer, if indeed she had understood what I was saying, the door opened and Jason walked in, better known as "J."

Jason is about six foot tall and weighs around eighteen stone. A very proud African black guy. Married with two young children. A particularly reliable and dependable bloke.

He works for me, and with me, both as driver and a security operative. He is also a friend.

"You okay?" he asked, with an unusually worried look on his face.

"What happened?" I asked again.

"You got shot," he explained. "During the scuffle, the bastards shot you; they took a shot at me, but hit the car."

What the fuck was he talking about I thought, trying desperately to move some part of my anatomy to confirm I wasn't crippled, and what is that smell?

1981, the Falklands... Argentina had occupied the islands; at the time, we were on a training exercise in Borneo. A little warmer than the Falklands, but then I think most people would rather be warm than cold.

It was Thursday, just before lunch. The temperature must have been in the hundreds, 100 percent humidity and the place just full of flying and crawling beasties.

One of the nicest things about places like this is when you're in your sleeping bag, completely covered from head to toe. You have washed yourself in anti-beastie bite ointment, draped a mosquito net over your sleeping place. The sound of the jungle, the sounds of the beasties trying to get their fix of blood; the confidence you have that they can't get to you: it's a great feeling. It's like ultimate power.

In contrast, in some tactical situations, when you are trying to sleep on the floor, you can't use the smelly stuff to keep them off because you can smell it from five hundred yards away in the jungle. Your only defense is your Army-issue, green face veil. The buzzing sounds like the beasties are laughing in anticipation of you falling asleep and your face veil falling off. The noise in between the buzzing is the bastards washing their hands before dinner.

We had been there for about ten days, playing all sorts of games along the Barito River.

We were based near a large town called Banjarmasin, which, luckily for us heat dodgers, isn't that far from the Java Sea; those who have visited the area will know it is a great place for swimming, surfing and generally arsing about.

The first four days, we spent at the furthest point inland of the Kapuas River, which is fun if you're either a lizard or one of those stupid looking sand rats. It's ridiculously hot, humid, and the beasties are the biggest you will find anywhere.

I think it's fair to say, generally in our organization, no matter where we trained, if it was away from home, we would always find something to moan about. In reality, the experiences were great, even if sometimes...rather bizarre.

Joining the army, for most of us, had been a foregone conclusion since the later stages of military secondary school. Primarily, because most parents (well, mainly fathers in those days) had been, or were serving in the armed forces.

Now that is a funny environment to be in. British Forces Education Services schools! I'm not knocking them; they were, and probably still are, necessary. But they were so different from civilian schools back home in the UK.

The discipline was generally very strict, I think because service personnel were expected to accept strict discipline themselves. Well, obviously in those days it was. Bit different now! I was not the perfect pupil, I have to be honest. If I could get away from doing anything that didn't appeal to me, I would–ranging from attending the first lesson and then climbing the fence and disappearing for the day, to just plain and simple not catching the school bus in the morning.

We had a dedicated school bus. It was an old thing painted green, as were most things involving the army in those days. We would get on the bus, travel for an hour to school. There must have been around thirty pupils per bus, and the buses came from about twenty different areas. I mean, people were shipped from all over the place to get to secondary school.

Of course we got caught, all of us.

We were shoplifting in a large German supermarket, nothing serious in our opinion at the time. I think we had a couple of flick knives, a starter pistol, and a load of fishing kit spread among eight of us. I remember the Germans used to nickname shoplifting 'Englisch Einkaufen,' meaning 'English Shopping.' Get the impression that we were pretty busy?

Anyway, this German store detective grabbed one of the other lads by the arm. As sons of the great British Army, we wouldn't accept that kind of behavior from these lowly German civilians. I can't remember the lad's name, but I remember him punching the store detective square on the nose. The store detective immediately let go.

We ran from the shop using the most direct route back to school. Over the chain-link fence, topped by barbed wire. We hid our ill-gotten gains in areas which were never frequented by anybody but us, and then we all dispersed to various ends of the school.

The school was an enormous place. It was contained within a British Army barracks; I think it was called Mansergh Barracks. If I remember correctly, the artillery were based there. It was also a pretty secure place.

Nevertheless, as we all walked back to our school buses at 1630 hours, ready to go home, there was this air of silence when a German policeman, a rather bloody-nosed-looking store detective, three military policemen, and a couple of guys in combat gear stood by the buses waiting for us.

I always remember my dad's saying. "Don't care what you get up to, but never bring the police to my front door!" Oh, dear!

I don't think he was overly bothered about us breaking the law; it was the inability to do something and get caught. "Shows a lack of backbone or spirit," he would say. Don't get me wrong, he was by no means a bad man, hard, but not bad. I dread to imagine what he would have become had he not joined the army.

For most of us, joining the army seemed the easy part.

As many squaddies will tell you, getting into the appropriate regiment, or getting out of the army once in was the hard bit. We all had the opportunity in those days of signing for either three, six, or nine years. You know, I can't even remember what I signed for. See, I thought it was part of life, joining the army, not a job! Strange, the differing perspective of soldiers who come from Civvi Street, and have seen what life is really about.

We were lucky, although we were moaning like fuck about the heat and humidity, the beasties and the smell…we were exactly where we wanted to be!

The RSM (Regimental Sergeant Major) called a meeting. He was as blunt as ever. "Right boys, we're off to the Falklands…" he said, grinning.

There was the usual silence when the RSM made a statement. With anticipated regularity, he would give us what we had come to accept as the hammer, followed by a long pause for his statement to sink in, then give us the nails, or the main ingredient of his announcement.

(This is not the SAS. As with the history of the SAS, until recent events this military organization has always been nameless. Thought I should clear that up before we go much further. See, I am not going to be an alias 'Chris Ryan' or 'Andy McNab.' I am telling you a story. From that story, many people will find extracts that they know to be true. Others will find extracts that they wish were not true, and the majority will hopefully just enjoy the story.)

We were a group of twenty-one men, a variety of ages, creeds, and colors, each one of us selected for a specific reason.

Everyone thought he knew the reason he had been selected, but in reality, it probably had nothing to do with why they had chosen us. See, in the SAS, you volunteer; they choose dependant on your performance over the selection course, etc. In the S.I.S., you are selected because of your already proven ability to achieve a large number of objectives, thus already fulfilling the requirements.

Well, I thought I knew why I was there–young, enthusiastic, not scared of much (except the fucking beasties).

In reality, later in life, those that survived would find out why!

Nobody ever spoke between the RSM's hammer and nails, as we had all experienced his temper, all knew not to steal his bit of thunder.

The RSM, John (or Jossie when he wasn't about)–Jossie referring crudely to a jock strap was obviously Scottish, born and bred in some slum in Glasgow. After a bottle (or two) of Scotch, he would quite regularly give us the brash version of his upbringing, well, 'up-dragging,' to be more precise. Mind, don't all Scottish ex-Special Forces guys claim to have had it harder. They all seemed to have had it so much harder than us fickle English chaps...yeah, right.

He must have been 5'7" and about fifteen stone, weight obtained through his obsessive eating of boiled potatoes with butter. He had sharp blue piercing eyes and incredibly white skin. I think it must have been trendy or manly to have a moustache back then, as the majority of guys had them, mostly unkempt small black rugs strewn across the top lip, trying really hard not to resemble Freddy Mercury.

I remember sitting, talking to him one day in the woods in Germany, whilst he patiently peeled twenty potatoes. Cracking sunshine, slight breeze, the usual circumstances to find someone in his position outside.

The army in BAOR (British Army of the Rhine), or squaddies based in Germany is probably a more familiar phrase, always seemed to spend exercises either in the woods and villages of Germany or the prairies of Canada. The poor Germans must have hated us.

There is nothing more off-putting than having a convoy of heavy Artillery travelling through your peaceful village at 0300 hours, trying to find a farm yard, not only to park up in, but also to dig holes, shit in, cook in, etc. Mind you, the subsequent rewards for the German farmers made things a little easier.

I think the amount of compensation paid to farmers for buildings that were allegedly damaged during NATO exercises could have re-built the majority of Germany!

I remember on numerous occasions listening to farmers discussing which particular building could do with being damaged by the next passing 432 (armored personnel carrier). A quick flick of the tiller (the steering mechanism) and bang, one demolished barn. This always concluded in a tidy compensation payment from HM's government and a few hearty fresh breakfasts for the squaddies.

And sex....well, in abundance. I could never understand why pretty German village girls would want to shag the pants off some dirty, grotty squaddie who hadn't had a proper wash for weeks.

Maybe the local male population wasn't up to scratch? I think it's fair to conclude that the villages probably needed fresh blood, to stop the cross breeding! No offense intended, of course.

Jossie would put the potatoes into one of those huge pans. The charity people use them for cooking food for starving Third World refugees. He would boil them in salt water until they were soft, then strain ten at a time, using a green army vest.

Loads of ex-squaddies will smile when I try to explain what an army green vest or army issue green Y-fronts were like.

The green vest was a string vest, mass-made for people of 7'6." Regardless of height, weight, or gender, everybody seemed to be issued the same size. The unfortunate guys under six feet had either a lot of spare material for making face masks or a lot of spare material to sit on...but, whoa betide if you were found not to be wearing one.

The Y-fronts were the same, the knackers' bit hung down to your knees combined, well. You can imagine the laughs we had catching each other walking around in them. I must admit though, once we left training, I never saw anyone wearing either…ever!

After putting the potatoes in the pan, he would throw in a whole wedge of Lurpack slightly salted butter. I mention the butter so distinctly because it was one of those items we could buy loads of, and unbeknown to the British tax man, it wasn't available to the Germans. Thus we made loads of dosh selling it to them.

I watched with admiration as he put the lid on this huge pan and tipped it up and down until he was satisfied the butter had melted. He ate eight full-sized potatoes with his fingers, directly from the pan. I thought he would burn his mouth out, but hey, no such luck!

He wrapped the rest in a newspaper. I asked what else he was going to eat; he just shook the newspaper at me.

Then came the nails.

"Topper, Marty, Mick, Jumbo, and Spike, you will be leaving tomorrow, first flight. You will travel back to the UK, get cleaned up and draw the necessary. Then onward. I'll brief you separately later."

"Draw the necessary" generally meant, once we had been briefed, we would be able to select whatever equipment we thought would be appropriate. Obviously not too much, but definitely never too little.

Some lads would think what a great opportunity to get loads of newly designed stuff, and make life really easy for yourself. But we were always taught to remember that whatever you took with you you would have to carry! So, for the budding Rambos, I'm afraid, little is great in the world of selfishness.

I had known Marty, Mick, Jumbo, and Spike for some time. In fact, I had known Spike since joining the artillery, the first regiment I was involved with when I originally joined the army–great family, Unit 23 (Gibraltar 1779 – 1783) Field Battery Royal Artillery. I knew it well. It was one the last units my father served in before leaving. He got posted there because of a broken neck he suffered in the Paras. I can still remember the hassle he caused by refusing to swap his maroon Para beret for a black artillery one. Proud old get!

Spike was the battery physical training instructor. He was responsible for assessing everyone on fitness tests and stuff like that. He will always be remembered in the artillery as being different.

I remember he always used to dress up strange, or so was the perception in those days. He would wear earrings, which was taboo. Have his hair dyed…also taboo, wear makeup–very taboo and then go off on his own to nightclubs that were frequented by people that took drugs…naughty, naughty!

As a mate, he was a great guy. Always helpful, always ready to give a hand, especially if you were married.

His accomplice, Tommo, was less weird, but equally as fit. More senior and slightly more sensible.

I worked with them in the gym for a year or so. It was great fun. I remember we were entitled to wear white t-shirts, well, vests really, with red edges on the arms and neck. Once you passed your AIPTI (Assistant Instructor, Physical Training Instructor) Class III course, you were also entitled to wear a badge on your chest, crossed swords I think it was.

There were quite a few good lads there at the time. Quite a few who I learnt a lot from. Paul Airey, I think he subsequently went off to jail. Some tosser had had an affair with his Mrs. Not only had he dishonoured the guy by sleeping with his wife, but the idiot then went to the local pub where Paul and some of the others were drinking, to rub his face in it. No wonder Paul stuck his face in the deep fat fryer. Would have gotten more had it been me. Yes, really good lads! I initially worked in the office, which was a ball.

It was like a small central control center. Everything of secrecy, confidentiality, and blackmailing value was kept there.

Leave, or holiday as it would be known in the real world. All servicemen were entitled to a free flight home to the UK once a year and train warrants for use when they got back to the UK. Everybody was entitled to a certain amount of leave. It was twenty-one days a year if you were based in the UK and twenty-eight if based in Germany.

In the office we used to record all leave warrants and flights on a leave card. It was great. All records were done in pencil.

The amount of cash we generated by selling extra leave, issuing extra warrants and flights was phenomenal. The guy who taught me, Roy, stayed in the artillery until the end of his twenty-two years and made it to sergeant major!

I suppose it was a bit of a financial suicide mission when I changed jobs and went to work in the gym.

Spike taught remedial PT. Those that failed to pass the Battle Fitness test or BFT as it was called would have to attend remedial PT after work and on a Sunday.

Battle Fitness test is the basic fitness test that all servicemen had to pass in order to be judged fit to fight. It wasn't that difficult. You would run in boots, lightweight trousers, a red t-shirt and puttees (cloth things that wrap around the top of your boots like gaiters). The first mile and a half we would run in a squad, so if there were sixty taking part, there would be three in the front, followed by another three and so on until you reached sixty. Everyone was required to keep in step for the duration. Once we had run a mile and a half (within fifteen minutes), the PTI would ask everybody to stop, turn around and then run back in an individual best effort; however, in under ten and a half minutes! Anything after that was a fail. I think the idea was that extra PT would get them fitter, and the policy at the time involved every serviceman having three chances of passing the Battle Fitness test. If you failed the third time, you were sent for a medical and faced the possibility of being medically discharged from the army....I never knew of anyone who was medically discharged from the Army. In those days, there was always an alternative.

I remember turning up to assist one day. He had a class of around twenty guys. Those that had failed usually failed because they had either drunk too much the night before, or were so bored with the army that they had become grossly overweight on alcohol. Either way, they were made to suffer. The exceptions to the rule were generally chefs, store men, and office workers. Chefs, because you were given better food than the others for giving them an easy ride; store men, because you never went short of equipment; and office workers, because you always had access to free flights and extra leave. Oh and the bosses of course, because life was worth living.

The class were all lined up in good military fashion, all wearing the issue red t-shirt, knee length, blue issue shorts and black plimsolls.

Each individual had a medicine ball in front of them on the floor. For those that are not familiar with a medicine ball, trust me, they are awkward to carry, heavy, and the worst thing to be confronted with in the gym.

"Pick up the medicine ball," he shouted. "Hold the medicine ball at arm's length out on front of you. Turn to your right. And...jog."

"Fucking what," I thought to myself.

He was a real twat with the fatties. But then again, I suppose, in the army in the good old days, things were different, and rigorous punishments were normal, unless, of course, people were clever enough to ask for an alternative.

In fact, before that guardsman cried bully in the eighties, things were pretty straight forward in the army when it came to discipline and bullying...or 'sorting out the pecking order' is a better expression than bullying. Even racism. We had never heard of it. Regardless of race, we all got along. I can honestly say that racism is one subject that never crossed my mind and was never mentioned by anyone. So thank you again, Mr. Politician!

When I arrived in Lippstadt, I was seventeen. I had lived there for most of my life with my parents. Lippstadt had been my father's second-to-last posting prior to leaving the army. He was remembered by all and sundry as being a stroppy bastard.

I had a girlfriend, Donna. I had known her for quite a few years. I think I had one of those juvenile 'love' things with her. Funny actually. We all remember the embarrassing moments in our sexual self education. I tried to have sex with her, from the front, with her jeans pulled to her knees. What a farce. It must be physically impossible unless your dick is over two feet long. But I tried for about five minutes, until she decided I had had too much to drink. Well, I can now formally admit I hadn't had a drink at all! All part of the learning curve, I suppose.

It was a scary place at seventeen. A very big and scary place. If you had any inhibitions, they were quickly exposed and dealt with.

I remember being out late one night; I must have been in the regiment for about two weeks. I arrived back in the barrack block around 0200 hours. Our block was about halfway through the barracks. Considering the place was full of around four hundred squaddies, I still found it to be a spooky place, particularly when no one was around. The walls were that thick, you couldn't hear people snoring or playing music, even in the next room.

To my dismay, Terry Farrow and Neil Stapleton were waiting for me at the top of the stairs. Terry was the battery heavyweight boxer. He was enormous! Stapes was also into boxing, I think, but he was a ginger-haired, wiry type of guy.

To this day, I'm not sure if I was frightened to death because I hadn't expected to see anybody, or because I had heard all those rumors of what they did to the new guy. Probably similar to what a new inmate feels when he first goes to prison.

As I got to the top of the stairs, Terry stood directly in front of me. "Where the fuck have you been?" he bellowed, obviously a little worse for wear through alcohol.

"To my bird's," I replied, probably with a little girlie squeak in my voice.

Stapes got a hold of me by the throat and pushed me against the wall. I remember Terry putting his face against mine and kept repeating, "Bird's...bird's...bird's."

For a minute it felt as though I was in a looney bin; they were fucking mad!

Stapes then put one of those disposable lighters to my face, and continued the chant, "Bird's, bird's, bird's!"

It's funny to look back on. I mean, today, if someone did that to you in the army, the repercussions would be amazing, but in the seventies and eighties, it was accepted as just fooling around.

Then they just stopped.

"Is she fit then?" asked Terry, in a placid friendly voice.

"Yes," I replied.

"Have you shagged her?"

"Yes," I lied, knowing damn well the truth would have made me a laughing stock.

"Good lad, now fuck off to bed," said Terry.

See, in the real army, it was more of a form of acknowledgment that you actually existed and to report it to the bosses would have been unthinkable. To discuss it and laugh about it amongst your colleagues was acceptable, even when your colleagues discussed and laughed about it with the two guys involved. But report it as bullying, no way.

I always remember they never bothered me again, in fact they were always friendly…I had become part of the family. And I mean it, regiments, sub-units, companies, sections, whatever the corp in the army, they were all families, they were great.

Even formal disciplines were real.

I remember being caught drunk at work, which was rare for me as I never really drank much. We had been on the town drinking German beer. God only knows why, I knew I could only manage three or four before I was pissed.

The following morning at 0800 hours, I staggered down the stairs. I had missed breakfast in the hope that the extra half hour in bed would make me feel a little better. It didn't. Without breakfast, I must have stunk of beer. I wandered down the corridor towards my office.

The boss called me in. The BSM (Battery Sergeant Major) called me into his office. All offices seemed to have the same layout: boss's chair, desk in front, another chair in front of that, which we were never allowed to sit in. Loads of military memorabilia hung around the room, with the statutory photo of us all framed on the wall directly next to his desk.

"You're fucking drunk," he screamed.

Now, in my later life, particularly in the military police, we learnt that in order to establish that someone was drunk–except for drunk driving, which obviously involved breath tests, etc.–you would have to state that the person involved had glazed eyes, walked with an unsteady gait, and smelled of alcoholic liquor; thus this constituted him being drunk.

"Yes, sir," I replied, apprehensively.

"Do you want to be charged and have your record fucked up already?" He continued to scream.

"No, sir," I replied, shaking.

"Well, you know the score then, don't you?" he continued.

Without having a clue what he was on about, I agreed.

Without further adieu, he came from around his desk walked to within two feet of me.

It appeared, as a young soldier, everybody above the rank of sergeant seemed massive. Not just their ego, but physically, too.

He punched me. I assume it must have been a right hook on the side of the head.

When I came round, he was sitting behind his desk, laughing. He stood up, leaned over his desk and asked, "Well, why the fuck are you still in my office?"

That was fair discipline in those days, and hence the reason so many servicemen have clean records.

With the exception of Marty, everyone else I knew I had met since joining the unit. Marty was a black Irish Catholic. He nicknamed himself Mandingo, for reasons understood by everyone.

The first time I met him was in Belfast, probably about eighteen months prior to getting 'nominated' to join the unit. We had been carrying out CP (close protection) duties in Belfast for some knob-head, who was probably number 9999 on the IRA's hit list.

We had stopped in the pub opposite the Olympia Hotel for a couple of glasses of Coke (really!). I noticed this black guy at the end of the bar; he appeared to be staring at us. I suppose at the time, he seemed unusual as it was pretty rare to find blacks in this particular bar. I was with a guy called John Clooney. Bit of a prick, but fit and knew his stuff when it came to CP jobs.

I said to him, "Is it my imagination, or is that black guy at the end of the bar eyeballing us?"

"I noticed that, too," he replied.

I put my pint…I mean my Coke down on the bar and walked toward the end where the black guy was staring. Fortunately, the toilet was directly behind him, so I wasn't necessarily acting suspiciously.

As I walked adjacent to him, he turned to his side and said, "Keep walking. I'll speak to you in the toilet."

I must admit, I was scared shitless. I thought he either intended to whack me (kill me), or he was a shit stabber who wanted to shag me (gay).

As soon as I entered the toilet, I drew my 9mm Browning from my under arm holster, cocked it, and put the safety catch on. I put it into my suit trouser pocket, with my hand firmly attached to the pistol grip.

The door opened quickly behind me. The black guy came straight toward me, staring right into my eyes. I instinctively pulled the pistol from my pocket and pushed it up into his face.

"Just breathe and I'll blow your fucking brains out, you prick," I said rather apprehensively.

"Okay, okay. Calm down," he replied.

I spun him around, pushed his face against the tiled wall and punched him as hard as I could in the kidneys. I still had the pistol in my hand. As he tried to slip down onto the ground, I grabbed him by the scruff of his neck and again pulled him up against the tiles.

"Who the fuck are you?" I asked.

He struggled to catch his breath.

"I asked you a question," I said with clenched teeth, preparing to hit him again.

"I'm with DET," he spluttered.

I paused for a minute.

"Charlie, Romeo 619," he gasped.

I immediately recognized the call sign.

"Why didn't you say something?" I said sympathetically, trying to turn him around and smarten his jacket.

I felt a right cunt!

He stared at me. "Because I noticed that one of the local players had followed you into the bar, and was speaking to a couple of other guys, who were obviously sussing you out."

He didn't seem too pleased.

"Ah, right." I spent the next few minutes apologizing.

"You must be Topper," he said, with a knowing smile.

"And how would you know that?" I asked with surprise.

"Your reputation precedes you, you fucking psycho."

Charming, I thought.

We planned in detail how to deal with the immediate problem. Funny though, every time we reached a critical point in the plan, he would say, "Don't worry. We will handle that bit."

Don't get me wrong; in those circumstances you enjoy it when someone else takes responsibility for something that seems so dangerous.

Upon returning to the bar, I saw that John was in deep conversation with an English-speaking bloke. Little did we know who the guy was.

"Ah, Topper, let me introduce you to Mike. He is an ex-squaddie, married a local girl, and has since settled here."

Anybody with any experience of Northern Ireland will tell you that, regardless how English you sound, nobody would have, in their right mind, admit to have being an ex-squaddie, married to a local.

"Nice to meet you," I said calmly.

"Who was the black guy?" asked John in front of his new friend.

"Don't know, I think he left. Talking of leaving, I think we should go to our meeting point at the Chinese. Don't forget, we're meeting those RUC tossers for a pint before we go for a meal."

John looked at me strangely, but quickly picked up on the point.

"Fancy coming for a pint?" I asked his new friend.

"Yes, I will. You go on ahead, Ill just ring the misses and tell her I'll be late." (No mobile phones available in them days!)

"Where exactly shall I meet you?" he asked.

"First pub you come across past the Chinese up the road," I told him.

We left and walked calmly up the road toward the Chinese restaurant. As we passed, I saw the black guy drive past, with another three guys in the car. Behind him was another car with another four guys inside. I felt somewhat more comfortable all of a sudden.

"What are we doing?" asked John.

"I think your new friend is working for the fucking IRA, and our friend at the bar was DET. I suppose it's fair to say we have walked into some shit, and they feel we have an obligation to help them clear up the mess. Just go along with everything I say, only shoot when I do...and in the same direction, and all should be fine!"

Just before we reached the pub, a small alleyway seemed an ideal place to wait for our new friend...and his friends, to arrive.

The alleyway was poorly lit, but was long enough to see the light at the far end. Hopefully there wasn't anything untoward lurking in the darkness. We moved far enough in so they wouldn't see us when walking by. God knows where the black guy and his chaps had gone. There they were…John's new English friend and yes...three new mates.

His mates looked like typical nomads. But, in Northern Ireland, one of the first things you learn, usually the hard way, is that you can never judge a person by his appearance.

They were all yappering away, obviously excited at what they were expecting to be an easy hit. Once they passed us in the alley, I started to walk out. They all stopped outside the pub and were looking through the window to see if they could see where we had sat. All three were looking. Bit careless, bit naïve.

I noticed the black guy and three of his colleagues approach them from behind. They were all armed. Quietly, effectively, and very professionally, all of the group were pulled away from the window, restrained, and pushed towards us at gunpoint. We moved them back into the alley where we had been hiding.

Out of the darkness came a shadow. It seemed huge. Everybody seemed to freeze.

"All right boys," said the person, in a broad Northern Irish accent. The guy emerged from the darkness. He was wearing an RUC uniform and appeared to be doing up his trousers. "I wasn't sure whether I should come out or not. I didn't want to blow your wee operation," he said.

"What the fuck were you doing," I asked.

"Come out here, ya stupid bitch," he shouted, looking behind him into the darkness.

Out strolled a beautiful young blonde. She still had her blouse open so we could just glimpse her breasts. We all laughed. The copper tipped his head as he walked away with the girl.

We searched them and found only one had a handgun, an old Smith and Wesson six shooter, loaded and as lethal then as it had been when new.

"And what is this for then, chummy?" asked the black guy. "Going to shoot your new friends, were you?" He thrust the gun into the face of the alleged English ex-squaddie.

"No, no, we weren't," he stammered. "We were just carrying it for protection." However, he no longer sounded quite so English; in fact, his accent was now broad Belfast.

"You cunt," shouted John, obviously upset at the thought of getting plugged in the bar by his new friend.

A white van screeched to a halt at the end of the alley. Another of the black guy's colleagues got out of the van and came toward us.

"No room in the cells," was all he said, and then walked back toward the van.

I was a little confused to say the least.

There seemed to be a strange, knowing silence about what he had said. He opened the rear of the van, walked around to the front, and got back into the driver's seat. It was strange. The whole atmosphere seemed to change. Instead of it appearing as a successful operation that would subsequently be celebrated, it seemed a lot darker. Nobody was smiling, as they had been. Nobody was speaking. It was all a bit eerie.

The four Irish guys were plasticuffed and gagged. They were then loaded, well, thrown into the van. We were told to get in with them, and not to talk.

This was getting spookier by the minute.

The rear doors slammed shut. It was dark. The front of the van had been cordoned off with some form of wood, painted black. We were driven for around forty minutes. There was absolute silence. We came to a halt.

The back doors opened and the black guy stood at the rear looking inside. He told us to get out and bring the others with us. One of the captives started whimpering, as though he knew something bad was going to happen.

There were seven of us altogether, and the four Irish.

"What are we doing here?" I asked. We seemed to be somewhere up in the hills. I think they call it the Black Mountains. We had been warned on our briefings to stay away from places like these. I thought it was because of the IRA.

"Shut up and watch," replied the black guy.

One by one, he marched the Irish guys to the side of a steep embankment. The other side of the embankment was almost a sheer drop. Once they were all lined up, I suddenly realized what was happening.

"Have any of you bastards got anything useful to tell me, or anything that you think will save your lives?" he shouted. He walked along the line pretty nonchalantly, whispering to them as he walked along the line. His face was tense; he kept gritting his teeth.

Nobody spoke.

"Ah, well! All for the cause, eh!" he shouted at them all. He put his Glock with silencer to the back of the first guy's head. He turned to us and smiled. Each of their heads snatched forward as he pulled the trigger. After each time, he put his foot into their backs and shoved them over the embankment.

I was amazed. I had just watched him kill them all in cold blood. I didn't know what to say. "They're still plasticcuffed," I blurted out.

The black guy laughed. "That's what I like to see, somebody who thinks on their feet. Everyone will think it was an IRA punishment squad. That's if the IRA admits to this happening."

I never saw him again after that until I joined the unit at its training center.

I had learnt a really important instruction from the RUC. I now knew what 'No room in the cells' meant.

Chapter Two

Life is all about perception. If you perceive something is wrong, or dangerous, or could result in your incapacitation, or worse, you will always feel a reluctance to do whatever the thing is.

I felt like that about things until I left the artillery. I was relatively normal. Things happen in life that change one's perception and thus, we change our whole approach to life. I suppose, in contrast, we rarely realize the impact some of our actions will have upon others until we actually experience the impact ourselves. I always felt that squaddies tend to have a great laugh winding each other up and others. Sometimes these wind-ups go a little further than anyone expects and thus people get hurt...emotionally rather than physically, but all the same, hurt.

Emotional pain has a tendency to last a lot longer than physical.

After leaving the army, I met a few people that seemed as though they barely had any realistic emotion. By that I mean they didn't seem to react as we would expect to situations that we would have found either upsetting or annoying. It's generally at such points in friendly relationships that you realize that you don't really know the person.

I think the greatest example is politicians and voters. I mean, we all know that politics in the UK is a load of bollocks. In actual fact, politicians don't really give a toss about what voters think about them until the elections are imminent. Let's be honest. We have them yapping on about family values and such like. Yet in the UK, we have a massive amount of people getting divorced. How many politicians are divorced and thus how many of them understand the divorce process? How many politicians have children from previous relationships and thus, when they talk about what is in the best interest of single parents, how do they know? Aha, they don't! They are all from the same ilk, all with similar education and all fucking liars!

But without an alternative, what do we do? I'll tell you what, we vote them back in. In doing so, we condone this emotionless future, this being governed by people who don't have any experience of 'real life' and we accept their decisions on our futures. Democracy is supposed to be the will of the majority. That being the case, why don't we vote on the government's decisions? I don't mean four years later in the general election, I mean before the decision is implemented. You know why? Because they know that we wouldn't allow half the crap they promote to be voted in.

I think Tony Blair is okay. I'm a conservative, but I think he is okay. I don't think I like the idea of that Gordon Brown guy though, he looks like a lazy, arrogant twat. When Tony Blair goes, it must be time for a general election.

Anyway, I start to lose track!

Ah yes, Borneo. I didn't pay much attention to the rest of the brief. I felt acutely aware that we four had drawn what would eventually turn out to be the very, very short straw.

Forty-eight hours later, I walked into my parents' house in the north of the U.K. We lived in a place in between Wigan and Liverpool, called Dalton, a place I'll never forget because my father is buried there. Can't miss his headstone, it's the one with Pegasus engraved on it…showing his love for the parachute regiment.

My father, himself ex-services, was sat in his usual chair, feet up and the statutory cup of steamy tea, lovingly made by my mother, proudly on the fireplace.

His chair was one of those reclining things, the ones on some sort of pedestal which spins around and things. It was a sort of checked, tartan thing, which we had bought him when he hadn't been well.

He was a great guy for those of us that understood him. Proud of his family and we, his boys, "in the eyes of anyone else," could do no wrong. He was about 5'7", stocky with a typical ex-services belly. He had his hair cropped short, either a number one or two, I think, because the use of the long fringe to hide the lack of hair had long since gone out of fashion. Not that he gave a toss about fashion…trust me...he just thought it looked significantly smarter, and more self disciplined.

I used to find the vest thing quite funny. He always seemed to wear a string vest at home, and was constantly rubbing his belly. It was as though he was proud of it. Nowadays, I spend half of my time holding mine in to try and hide the mid-life spread, or wear slightly baggier shirts to hide the same.

Whilst most guys of our ilk have the same issues, I'm one of those vain bastards that hate it.

My dad! What a guy. No vanity, 100 percent man.

In our later years together, I told him just about everything that had gone on in our lives, except one thing. There was one thing I kept from him, as I knew in his deteriorating health, he would go ballistic and probably cause himself some severe grief.

My brothers nearly died when they found out that, one drunken night, when we were on our own–my father, mother, and I–I had grassed on my brothers.

I had gone through life allowing my parents to believe that I was the only one really to get into bother as a child. They were quite surprised to hear the truth. We had all been as bad as one another, just I was always the one to get caught. As they had never gotten caught, they excelled in school, and thus went onto their preferred careers.

There was only one thing I could never tell Dad. I think I told my brother Andrew once, whilst under the influence. We lived in a place called Blamford Cottage in Farnborough. My father was stationed with seven Para RHA. He was away a lot, generally on active service fighting the Arabs (even then!), or on military exercise, practicing for the next conflict. Mostly Northern Ireland though.

Our home! Fantastic place, right in the middle of the woods. In those days, there was a single carriage road opposite (which is now a dual carriageway). Behind was a large building, I think called government house. We had an absolute ball in the woods. I mean, as kids, who wouldn't! The Parachute Regiment depot (training unit) used to run their baby soldiers behind the house and into the woods. They were great. Always pleasant and fun.

My parents used to go out quite regularly to functions, in fancy uniform (Mess Dress), and long dresses. Yes, Dad in the uniform, and Mum in the dress...just in case you wondered! Therefore, they would have some guy babysit. I was six.

I remember being in bed one night and waking to some funny noise. We all slept in the same bedroom. I instantly needed to go to the toilet. I always found that, as a child, if you woke up, you needed to go to the toilet.

As I walked out of the bedroom door, I saw somebody rushing into the toilet. I remember for a moment being very scared. Instead of going back to bed, I went to the toilet. To my relief I saw it was the babysitter. He was stood over the sink.

I asked if I could go to the toilet. And he obliged with a smile.

It's that trust thing that kids have. He was the appointed babysitter, he was obviously trustworthy. Whatever he said went!

At the time, it didn't mean anything to me, but I remember he had his penis in his hand over the sink. I remember he had an erection.

I went to the toilet. I had to brush past him to get to the toilet. He stood there for the duration, watching me. I know I wasn't scared of him, as I never really had any reason to be. He had always been pleasant to us all.

Once I had finished, he was still standing at the sink. He seemed to be in pain, either that or he was doing something I couldn't relate to.

He told me to go into my mum and dad's room. He was smiling.

I was a bit worried about this as it was one of those cardinal sins to go into our parents' bedroom.

He assured me it would be all right. I went. It was dark. He followed me in. I never had any pajama bottoms on.

He told me he was going to be nice to me, but it might hurt a little. You can imagine the rest....although hopefully not. I lived in fear for years of him telling my dad, as he said my dad would kill me if he found out. I even started to wet myself in school when thinking of the consequences.

I never told!

Anyway...for one reason or another, the guy died in a serious accident in 1985. He was so badly injured he was hardly recognizable. I think I was on a course at the time...you can check it in my police statement. See, perception again. So from an early age, I became one of those guys that hated pedophiles, and no matter what the government or law says, if I have the opportunity, I would gladly help them in reducing the numbers that saturate our jailing system.

Where was I?

Ah yes, I had arrived home.

As usual, he barely raised his head, "All right mate," he called, engulfed in a western movie on the television. He was good, hard working, proud, angry bastard, my father.

I remember hating him as a kid, for the beatings, the discipline, and the arrogance. Although, now my brothers and I look back and laugh about most of it. There were always three of us brothers, all around two years apart. My eldest brother, Adrian, was quite sensible as a kid; I always thought of him as a giant. I could never really relate to him though; I would refer to him as some kind of family monster, even jokingly; we used to call him "The Thing." He was tall and had out-of-control dark hair.

Then there was Andrew, a real smart-arse. Never had to try, everything came naturally to him. Somehow, it was funny, he was also pretty tall, but had an Italian look about him.

We were all so different. Although it's hard to admit, I was the only really handsome one (ha-ha). I was also the cursed third son, crap at everything except making explosives, escaping from the police, shoplifting, and generally being a little shit. So, in retrospect, I suppose, one must accept that, based on family discipline in those days, most of the beatings and things might have been justified.

I remember my dad explaining to me that life would always be more difficult for me, being the third son. He had been third, but I think he was third from ten.

I remember one night when I was twelve, Adrian therefore about fifteen and Andrew, thirteen or fourteen. We had all gone to bed. Adrian slept in a single bed. Andrew and I shared bunk beds. Andrew was on the bottom bunk. The room was only semi-dark, as the curtains were drawn, but it was one of those light summer evenings. Remember those? When we used to have summers.

Our room was quite cramped. It was painted light blue with emulsion. The only window was directly above Adrian's single bed. The door was directly opposite the head of the bunk beds and so noise from the bunk beds could be heard from outside the room. In those days, swearing in earshot of an adult was a physically punishable offense.

Andrew kept putting his feet under the springs of my bunk and pushing me up in the air, which, whilst fun to start with, eventually started to make me feel sick. But, as expected from older kids, the worse I felt, the more enthusiastically he would kick. Adrian was fast asleep, probably dreaming about female things.

Just before the water from my stomach hit my mouth, I jumped off the bunk and dived on top of Andrew. I managed to get my knees on his shoulders and pin him down. I remember his exact words.

"Get off me you fucking prick," he shouted.

It was like some sort of magical spell. It was amazing. The door to the bedroom flew open and yes, my father happened to have been outside. He ran into the room as if he were on a mission. I climbed as fast as possible back up onto my bunk and into my bed, quickly dragging my sheets and blankets over me.

With his seemingly Mr. Universe strength, as quick as I had the covers over me, my father had them off again and he was slapping at me from every angle imaginable.

I knew it was my lucky night though; I was first. He then dropped to his knees and started beating the already weeping Andrew, and for the record, this is the only occasion in my childhood that I remember laughing whilst another was getting a beating. Then, the funniest thing.

He turned to "The Thing," all cozy and fast asleep, ripped the covers off him and shouted, "Don't you pretend you're asleep," and started on him. Well, I lay with my pillow stuffed into my mouth to stop him from hearing me laughing.

Old clever bright bollocks below me, as brainy as anybody you will ever meet, suddenly burst out laughing, which appeared not to impress my father much and to make matters even worse. As my father turned around to see what was so funny, he saw me with the pillow in my mouth. He was like a frenzied dog!

I think he gave up beating us after twenty minutes or so, as it had become hopeless. I must say, it was one of those times during a beating from my father I could honestly say, that was a laugh.

Anyway, my mother, typical seventies mum, loved us kids, spent most of her married life washing, cooking, and giving birth. She is a lovely lady and always greets us as though we has been away for years.

I think she had some idea what I was up to, but chose, through experience, never to bring it up. I was in Colombia when I was twenty-four, I think we were hanging around the Meta River area, playing games and sneaking across into Venezuela. (At this point of the book, American secret service agents take a deep breath! Don't worry, nothing exposed). I phoned her via satellite to see how she was; I told her I was in Canada. Only when I put the phone down did I realize I was surrounded by people speaking Spanish, but I knew she wouldn't have minded.

After the three boys came a sister...how weird, I was only four, but I distinctly remember her being born. Anything that meant my father had to look after us for any length of time was indeed significant and, therefore, memorable.

Poor girl, I think generally, she didn't have much to do with us boys. In fact I can remember distinctly the times where her presence made any difference at all.

Once on the stairs in the married quarters we were growing up in, in Lippstadt, a place in the midst of North Rhein, Westphalia, Germany, she asked me for some money. I must have been thirteen. I naturally told her where to get off. Again, she was only eight or nine. She said she would scream if I didn't.

I remember this being one of the first catch-22 situations in my life's experience and I was being taught it by an eight-year-old girl.

I laughed, she screamed, my father flew up the stairs.... I got a beating.... fuck, she was clever. I'm sure I'll remember the others later.

Chapter Three

Back to home in England.

Mum asked did I want some dinner and of course, it would have been stupid to refuse. She had already prepared a meal that would probably have fed five and, out of respect, you always finished the meal.

Funny actually, having spent so much time in the army, and coming from an army family, you tend to eat more than you necessarily need and usually quicker than others. I have always had a good appetite, hence my size in those days; I was six feet, weighed sixteen stone and carried a six-pack Arnie would have been proud of.

The meal was then followed by pudding with custard. You can understand why my father was always in his chair. The minute you stop exercising whilst eating like that, you explode in size. I left about 7:30 am, the following morning, got a lift to Liverpool from my eldest brother, who now worked there as a policeman...or 'a *busy*' as the local scousers would say.

I was met by the others at Speke airport. We boarded a Sea-King helicopter, one of those big strange-shaped ones that were used to do sea rescue jobs. We were flown back to our UK base.

The briefing was good, short, and to the point. One hundred times worse than anticipated. We were going to parachute into the fucking sea in the dark.

Obviously the planners didn't have a clue what it was like to parachute in the dark into cold water, bastards!

We were to set up Ops in preparation for the task force, which would be assembled and developed. We were, where possible, to reduce the enemy defense capability...without compromising ourselves. We were to have contact every forty-eight hours with D.1A, (MI6 control) via satellite phone. No other communications. No Medivacs. No re-supply. I sat staring into the abyss, thinking, calculating. I mean, reasonably speaking, how long would it take to assemble a task force of such magnitude to be able to take on the Argentinean Army? Don't get me wrong, I know they aren't exactly perfect soldiers, but, they do have a few Migs and missiles, as well as a well-populated rather large country a short spit away. Whereas, we, well, aren't exactly based on the island's door step and whilst we have a far superior army....and navy...and air force (got to keep the other chaps happy), it would take some organizing. So I guess we won't count on just being there on an overnight jolly. I started to look around the room. I think I may have been trying to find the entrance to Superman's phone booth, or the fucking Bat Cave. I mean, how the fuck did I get involved in this shit? Surely this was SAS territory, not ours.

I joined the army when I had just turned sixteen. As a squaddie's son, it was easy; we didn't have to go on these pre-selection courses. I signed on whilst at school. I signed on with the artillery.

My father went ballistic. "The fucking artillery. What is wrong with you?"

Anyway, eight months after signing on, I got off the train at Nuneaton, in Warwickshire, slightly apprehensive, expecting the worst.

This big, burly guy came over and asked, "You going to Bramcote, mate?"

I replied sheepishly, "Yes, I think so." Even as I answered, I felt the twinge of nervousness.

We were delivered to the barracks in a white minibus, driven by the same guy. God, it was scary.

I recall the drill square appearing to be an enormous tarmac area, where we would spend many a painful hour marking time. There were rows and rows of H blocks, where everyone would be accommodated.

We were escorted to the main hall, and then left in disorganized groups until they shouted our names and put us into troops. I was in Nicholson Troop.

First stop, the barber. Now that's when the reality hit home! That's when you saw the first of the tears. I couldn't believe people expecting to join the army with long hair, but I suppose as an army brat, I had always been used to short hair.

I spent a year in Bramcote. Some of it was funny; other stuff was boring. One particular incident comes to mind every time I think of Bramcote.

We were housed in large rooms; about sixteen per room, if I remember correctly. Eight per side of the room, with a metal, double-fronted locker each, placed strategically between each bed. We had four large rooms as bedrooms, so four by sixteen in the troop, one large shower room shared by all, ten sinks and six toilets. Oh, and one bath. It was never really safe to use the bath, as any form of undefended relaxation meant at least four bored baby soldiers would have time to dream up some sort of joke; either throw bleach or shit in the bath with you.

I suppose with basic military training, it's difficult to form an opinion of whether the accommodation is comfortable, as every hour spare is spent cleaning uniform, polishing boots, or sleeping the latter generally the more popular.

I befriended one guy in particular, from Manchester. Chris Reid.

He was quite slightly built, but all muscle. He was black and almost bald, not just due to the recruit's haircut. He very quickly became famous for his head butting.

Except for instructors, if anybody confronted him over anything, he tended to head-butt them. No notice, no chit-chat, just drop them. I was glad he was my mate.

Actually, talking about the one incident, it did involve him. Outside our block or accommodation, but in between three other blocks of the same size (so thus housing 4 x 16 baby soldiers), was but one BT pay phone.

The queue to use it at night was usually twenty to thirty guys long; and therefore telephone calls were short, unemotional and whispered.

I remember standing in the queue behind Chris (clever, see) and a large jock guy walked up the queue where he obviously had a friend who had been saving his place. Yes, I suppose it looked arrogant and confrontational, but surely not as bad as what he got for it.

Chris turned and shouted "Oi, fucker, where do you think you're going?"

The guy walked back towards us, and I thought *Oh no!*

He said, "My mate has been keeping my place, shit head, so fuck off!"

Out came the famous head-butt, but the guy didn't go down.

The line of people waiting for the phone almost immediately changed and formed a circle. I didn't see the knife; I honestly didn't even know he had one. Within seconds, no matter where it came from, it was stuck, all five inches of the blade, in the jock's stomach.

Chris let go, turned to me and said, "Time to go."

No emotion, no fear, just walked away.

I lay in bed that night, worried to death about what would happen, I was soon to find out.

My first encounter, as a soldier, with the dreaded RMP (Royal Military Police). The lights went on and two monsters in number two dress, with peaked caps stood at the end of our room.

One shouted, "Reid, Brown, get out of bed now!"

It's worse than they would have you believe, or it used to be–the army, that is. Well, until all that stuff about bullying and racism was splashed all over the papers. It's funny, I grew up as a soldier's son, joined the army thinking that intimidation and general violence toward other ranks was normal and expected. The military police, prior to the introduction of PACE (Police and Criminal Evidence Act 1984), were certainly a law unto themselves and the only time you would ever confront them in an aggressive manner was if you were drunk, accompanied by your mates.

There was some credit to be had as a squaddie being brought back to camp in the back of an RMP vehicle, unless they charged you, that is. The usual procedure was to receive a few slaps from them in the vehicle on your way back to camp. They would hand you over to your own boys in the guardroom and you would be required to sleep in a cell until six-ish. Then back to your room for the applause.

I stood to attention outside the guardroom in a pair of army green Y fronts, a pair of black issue plimsolls and a red PT vest. The guy on guard duty at the gate kept looking over, in either pity or disbelief at the way I was dressed. I was shaking. It didn't seem cold, although it was fresh. I guess I was worried. Chris had been taken straight through to the back rooms where he would have been having some form of initial interview.

I remember thinking, *what am I scared for... I haven't done anything wrong.... Why should I accept being treated like this? I'm going to go inside and say I'm not putting up with it!* The guardroom door opened and the RP (Regimental Police) Sergeant, Sergeant Dempsey came out. About thirty-five years old, dark hair, probably dyed, ugly as shit, ready for retirement but certainly not stupid.

He stood quietly in front of me and whispered, "You okay, son?"

"Yes sarge," I replied. I think it was the disbelief that under the circumstances somebody in authority could sound concerned that made me cry. The tears ran uncontrollably.

"Come on, get a grip," he said.

I sniffed and took a deep breath.

"Come inside, you can't stand out here like that," he said.

I followed him inside, behind the counter where all junior soldiers going out and back from town would have been paraded.

About 0615 hours, one of the RMPs, a corporal, came into the room. I was quite relaxed; the sergeant had made me tea and generally made me feel more confident.

"I told you to stand outside," the corporal shouted.

"And I said he could come inside," replied the sergeant.

"He is under my jurisdiction now, sergeant, so he will do as I say," said the RMP, bullishly.

The RP sergeant stood and stared at the inferior-ranked policeman with more authority and said, "Listen, you arrogant little scrotum; unless you arrest him he's in my guardroom, therefore I am responsible for him. Are you going to arrest him?"

"Well...no, he's a witness," replied the RMP.

"Well, fuck off back to your little room and when you're ready for a statement, ask me to make him available."

As the RMP left the room, I got the impression he wasn't very happy.

When I did finally go to give my statement, they were actually very friendly. They just wanted to know what I had seen.

I told them. "The guy pushed in on the queue for the phone. He and Chris rowed and Chris head-butted him. I didn't see a knife; I thought the guy had fallen because of the head-butt."

I was back in my room by 0900 hours. Everybody wanted to know what had happened, had they beaten me up, etc.

About two days later Chris reappeared in the block. He came up to me and said, "Thanks mate," and the matter was never mentioned again.

Chapter Four

After two stops of a few hours, I leapt from the doors of the Hercules plane into the darkness, immediately feeling the cold on my face and through our wonderful thermal jumpsuits. HALO jumps (High Altitude Low Opening) in the dark always gave me the willies. There was a full moon, which was helpful. A few minutes of joy, followed by the always grateful thumping of the chute opening, then searching for the sea.

I could see the shadows of the land, easily identifiable because the moon didn't reflect off it. Then, I held my breath; this was going to be cold. Funny, after about ten seconds, I let my breath out, and looked down thinking I had misjudged....splash! Typical, just when you're not prepared, it happens. I hit the water totally unprepared, and God, it was cold. A quick release and swam onto the shore. Fuck, I was cold! We had only been in the water for a few minutes; the cold water was a killer.

On shore, everybody dried off as quickly and quietly as possible, tied up gear, and checked things off. Nobody spoke. Within minutes we were ready and made for the grid reference where we were to make base. It took us around an hour. Fortunately, it turned out to be a cave. Not many of those around, let me tell you.

Mick was the team leader, thirty-one years old, half-Brit, half-Greek, about 5'9" tall, really rough complexion, straight black hair to his collar, weighed about fourteen stone, spoke with a slightly Yorkshire accent. His surname sounded Russian to me, but hey, what the heck, if he passed the vetting to do a job like this, he couldn't have been too closely linked to the commies.

I remember in the rare periods of downtime we had, he would also listen to music of the Brian Ferry ilk, and I think on the quiet, he thought he could sing a bit. Trust me, he couldn't

Spike, twenty-six, as I described earlier, was extremely fit. Slightly changed from his more controversial artillery days. Now he was more sensibly a communications expert, spoke loads of languages, natural blond-haired guy (dyed black for obvious reasons), about six feet, good-looking gigolo type, cockney.

Jumbo, 5'7", was the qualified combat paramedic, dark curly hair, Scottish, aggressive, about twelve stone, reliable to the hilt.

Marty was the oldest amongst us. He had spent most of his army career in the Paras. I think it was two Para. I always used to look twice at him. His hair should have been red or ginger. It certainly looked completely out of place being dark. Even his eyebrows were a different color. But he regularly assured us that he had never dyed it. Even clandestine searches of his locker proved negative in the illustrious hair dye operations.

And me.

We got inside the cave; surprisingly it was quite cozy, about thirty feet across, fifteen to the back, few sharp edges, very little dew. I think it was probably a little too cold and near to the sea for there to be too much wildlife. Mind you, we did hear some weird noises coming from the deeper parts of some of the caves further on. We had jumped into the sea to the east of Pebble Island and made our way to the coast just off Port San Carlos. The rest is confidential. The cave seemed as though it was heated once you got out of the wind.

Mick put his finger to his lips. "Sshhh." Silence. He burst out laughing

Spike looked at him and asked, "What's so fucking funny?"

Trying to catch his breath, Mick replied, "Did you see Topper hit the water?"

Bastard had noticed!

They all rolled around laughing (quietly). When they had finished, Spike and Mick decided to go off and identify the emergency RVs.

Jumbo and I went out and cleared the perimeters, set up a few claymores and drew a location diagram. I then started setting out kip or sleep areas, while Jumbo sorted out a brew and semi-prepared wood.

About two hours later the others returned. They had sorted all they needed to.

Spike said, "They're about three miles northwest of us. Probably between sixty to one hundred strong, three trenches each, double-manned."

"They don't seem prepared for anything, very relaxed, very easy," said Spike.

Time for sleep... well, two up, two down; two sleep four hours, then swap. Twelve hours later, fed, slept, out, ready to go.

"It's about 0220 hours, loads of time to go snooping," whispered Spike.

Three miles doesn't sound far, but four guys sneaking across rough terrain, rocks, water, and crap, carrying their kit, is quite challenging.

After an hour we stopped. Mick had a small hand-drawn map of where the trenches were, not that it was difficult to see them.

Shining torches, smoking, drinking beer, God! *They're on holiday,* I thought. I had never seen anything like it. For fuck's sake, even on training exercises in Germany, the British Army were 100 percent more vigilant than these bozos.

There were two guys per trench, obviously not anticipating anyone turning up this soon after their little invasion. The plan was quite simple really. Get in the trench, kill the occupants…quietly, then on into the next. Once all three trenches were dealt with, look what else was vulnerable.

Spike and I crept off, targeting the trench farthest off to the right. The others would stand by, in case we were compromised at any point. The trench was around about seventy yards in front of us. We had night vision, guns and knives…all personal choice. The two guys in the trench were both leaning over the front, so in effect, the opposite way from our approach. They were both smoking and chatting, and believe it or not, they had a small transistor radio wedged against a rock with music blasting out. I couldn't believe it.

Once directly behind them, simultaneously, we slipped into the trench, knives levelled at head height. Both guys turned at the same time, probably expecting their colleagues. Both of their weapons were on the side of the trench, probably not even loaded.

Ball of the hand under the chin, cover the mouth with the palm and fingers, cross the other hand with your knife so that the hand is underneath your other elbow. Pull the knife hand back so the blade enters the throat at a 90 degree angle, then pull both hands across, pulling the chin up and left with one hand and the knife into the throat and all the way across the windpipe, use your body weight to stop the struggle and wait.

The music from the first trench was still playing as we approached the middle trench. Even more fascinating. One guy was asleep outside the trench, lying on a foam mat; the other was listening to a Walkman and reading a book using a torch.

Once they were all dead, we took their dog tags from around their necks. We removed all of the bodies and piled them inside what appeared to be an old culvert, quietly filling it with rocks. I always found it really polite to take the dog tags. At least if the bodies couldn't be found, the parents or next of kin would know they weren't coming home. It was almost light when we finally finished burying the bodies and clearing up the trenches.

You see, with conscripts, when you put more than one or two guys together, the likelihood of them pissing off on a jolly, or going AWOL, is significantly increased than if one guy is on his own in a trench.

Jumbo decided he would record all the dog tag details, which would be handed over once we had concluded.

"Hey, 1966. How old does that make this guy?" he asked.

Well, it was 1981...God! Fifteen!

"For fuck's sake," he said. "These are almost fucking kids."

I don't think it was mentioned again.

Again, see, the perception of death at the time, it was wrong to kill juveniles, or kids. I suppose it didn't matter deep down that they were wearing uniforms and would most likely have shot us if they had ever had the opportunity. Not much life experience before death. Seems wrong somehow, but hey, a job is a job.

The Argies obviously weren't very bright. We went back a few nights later and carried out a similar little exercise and again met little or no resistance.

The night before the British task force was due we had a ball. Throughout the night we were attacking almost anything and everything. We attached explosives to all kinds of personal kit, vehicles, even in one case to a guy who was fast asleep. I also remember trying to wire this guy's rifle whilst he was asleep and then pushing the grenade into his boot. I taped another grenade to someone's helmet, the wire through one of his belt loops. Yes, that's how easy it was. They weren't even amateurs. Apart from the fun we saw in the morning, the rest is somebody else's history.

It's weird. Life is something very precious, and it's right that we should protect it. But in reality, the biggest risk to life is us. Yes, we humans are so hell bent on self destruction, you wonder sometimes why we spend so much time and effort finding cures for illnesses. The reason we have to get involved in a conflict is because we value life and want to preserve it. Hmmm.

Chapter Five

1991 again.

Been shot, eh? I couldn't believe it, Jason's face was pretty convincing though. I remembered starting this job; it seemed quite a challenge, sounded quite good. Estate Security. I thought the land owner was quite a nice guy. He didn't half inherit some shite from his uncle though, some of the old policies I mean. He seemed quite modern, with it and definitely in with the 'in' crowd. Whether that be the royals, the Beckhams or whoever was deemed to be 'in' at the time. His wife was very fit (the man's version of fit). Yes, she was fit, lovely face, lovely figure and what a personality. She was always astute, knew or wanted to know what was going on and, where she could, she loved to get involved.

It was strange really. The estate manager asked me if I would like to help sort out some of their security issues. *Well, of course I would,* I thought. Fabulous estate, twenty-five hundred acres within walls six feet high, a safari park, hell, it was certainly something new.

I had dealt with most things in my life, but not a safari park; although I had dealt with some wild animals.

I remember walking in Uganda in the early eighties, after the Falklands.

The boss had said, "Fancy a cushy number for six months?" which roughly translated into, "You're posted for six months, whether you like it or not!"

The Royal Military Police provided close protection duties throughout the world, looking after the embassies and ambassadors; they were pretty good at it. I had seen their training at Longmoor near Chichester; they were very thorough and convincingly professional. See, so not all RMPs were tossers. A necessary part of the job was to constantly carry your preferred firearm.

As old fashioned as it may seem to some of the modern sweats out there, my favorite was always the 9mm Browning. No, not even the HK. I liked it like a twenty-year-old bird. Close protection was pretty straight forward. Babysitting the big boss! We went there because the Home Office wanted an independent look into how things were working out in the embassies. Well, what a good idea, said some tit. Let's get some first-hand evaluation.

I was sent there for six months. How fucking boring!

After six weeks working in the embassy, a guy called Norman, or Norm, asked me, "Hey, Topper, fancy a bit of R and R with us?"

"Where to?" I asked apprehensively.

"Kenya," he replied. "We usually get flown into the hu-lu by chopper with all our gear and traipse around for a couple of weeks."

The hu-lu, or however one would wish to spell it, was a typical squaddie term for the outback, wilderness, desert, or anywhere that could be wandered across, played war on, or generally used by the services for exercise.

What about lions? Was my first thought. I tried to ask in such a way that I didn't show how scary I found the whole idea.

"Ah, don't worry," said Norm. "We'll take a couple of SLRs and a few nine millis. That usually keeps them away, plus it beats snaring."

I hoped the snaring was a joke.

It was May, if I remember correctly. So, whilst it's never really cold in Kenya, May tends to be the time when you usually have high grass, a bit of rain, but it's generally not too hot. So, off we went, mad, stupid, all those I suppose, but boy, it was fun.

We were dropped around eleven o'clock on Saturday morning. The flight over in a Chinook helicopter was an eye opener, especially watching the herds of animals flocking across the plains in fear of the unknown buzzing above.

There were five of us in total: Norm, John, Billy and Mal, all RMP's (Well, sort of). It was bizarre, after spending so many years exiting aircraft and running or adopting defense positions, the relaxed amble on exit, to the smiling pilot all seemed a bit too surreal. Our packs were especially light, probably forty to fifty pounds each, enough kit to be comfortable, but not necessarily clean. I actually remember sitting there with my pack thinking, "I'm really going to enjoy this."

We set off heading northwest from Voi, which is a cracking place! It was pleasantly warm, not too hot. The tracks along the way were some kind of reddish-colored clay, which funnily enough made the elephants in the area also a reddy color. It was strange, but distinguished them somewhat from all the elephants I'd seen elsewhere on my tours.

Talking of tours, one of my most bizarre postings springs to mind, coincidentally also in the eighties–Lebanon! Without all the fanatical grumpy bastards, it would have made a great tourist state; but with all those fanaticals, with their overactive sense of righteousness and constant bickering, no way would it be deemed to be a safe place for tourists. Ask Terry Waite. It's funny sometimes to see these guys with expectations that their religious reputations will be honored, even respected, whenever they go. We may love you, Terry, but trust me, they don't. They didn't give a toss. In fact, the forwarding of information to one specific person regarding the visit, gave them just the power they needed to plan the kidnap. What a fuck up!

We were sent there for six months as a CP team to look after the ambassador and the embassy. Sounded like fun to me, bit of babysitting, bit of sunbathing, maybe even some shagging. Lots of that went on between the American and British embassies, and why not, we love each other.

The safe building, in case of any emergencies, and where everybody slept and relaxed, was elevated behind the embassy's main building, with enough distance to safeguard the ambassador if the embassy was blown up. It was deemed far enough away to avoid the destruction of safeguarded material, off-duty staff, etc.

If the chaps on duty thought they were about to be attacked they simply pressed the button and everybody would be called upon to assist.

I remember the first night; after formal and informal introductions were over, the boss showed me around the secure area. There was this creepy, low-pitched alarm sound. As he didn't seem too concerned, I didn't acknowledge it. Between three to five minutes passed and it stopped.

"That bloody alarm," he said.

I asked him what it was. To my amazement it was the embassy attack alarm, which, according to protocol, all staff should evacuate to the safety of the secure buildings.

Later, I was explaining what happened to Spike, who burst out laughing. "He doesn't care if you throw a hand grenade under his table, he always believes if your time's up, accept it!"

"Oh fucking great, we've got a fucking hero to babysit!"

Give him credit though. As times were somewhat dodgy, he wasn't permitted to have his wife stay so, as every good English gentleman does, he had a mistress. She was based in the American embassy, but conveniently had plenty of hand deliveries to make. His wife was based in Cyprus.

Never the twain shall meet.

A formal dinner night was taking place at the American embassy; all ambassadors were invited, so obviously the boss had to attend. The American embassy is a multi-story, relatively high-rise building. Car parking is in a large underground car park, directly under the building. We used two vehicles with a one-and-three set-up: one CP in the lead vehicle with the ambassador and three in the rear.

The first vehicle was instantly permitted access by the enormous American marines standing inside the gates. We stopped and passed the usual friendly comments about the heat, glad there were so many of them on duty, etc.

The lead vehicles pulled up in front of the building with us closely behind. A marine in very pretty white gloves opened the door for Stratham (the ambassador), who thanked him and scurried off up the stairs, to be greeted by, amongst others, his favorite American ambassador.

We were armed with MP5s (machine pistols 9mm) and 9mm Brownings (automatic handguns), with enough ammunition to start a war.

All seemed calm enough.

I walked over to the lead vehicle, which had been driven by John 'C' (nicknamed Jesus). I leant over to talk to him. A truck approached the main entrance at high speed. Little was known in those days about suicide bombers.

They say when something really bad happens in your life, it usually appears to happen in slow motion. Well, fuck me, that *Matrix* film has fuck-all on this. The marines who were standing behind the gates were knocked for six. It seemed obvious the bomber was heading for the underground car park. If he had made it, in all probability the whole building would have come down, including crushing the six hundred people inside. Our weapons were always at ready when we left the Embassy, so I simply swung my MP5 around and put the whole mag through the cab window of the truck, as did the other two colleagues from the rear or cover vehicle.

The truck veered off slightly to the right and impacted against a side wall to the entrance of the car park. Then whoof! Up it went.

I'd never really flown before, well, outside of planes and things. The impact is like being hit all over at the same time by a hundred hammers. Luckily for us, it was literally just the blast that hit us, no debris.

When the dust started to settle, the devastation was obvious, but not as bad as it would have been had the truck made it into the car park. I think ninety were hurt, some quite badly, some critically injured.

Statham came out of the building and stood for a moment at the top of the stairs. "Some bang, eh," he said, looking me up and down, as if to be disappointed that I was covered in dust.

"How's things inside, sir?" I asked.

"I have no idea," he said. "I was busy going through some paperwork in one of the offices!" Well! The lucky bastard, he had obviously been with his 'bit on the side' when all the shit had gone off.

"I suppose the vehicle is not available for a lift back to the embassy then," he stated, rather than asked.

Coincidentally, the lead vehicle wasn't too bad, so he and three team members drove back to the safety of the British embassy. So cool, so controlled yet so very, very deadly!

Talking of weird people, weird decisions and things, I remember being in the RMP in the days when bullying, intimidation, and the recruitment of outright wankers was the norm. I mean, some RSMs of non-war units were so bored that they made life hell for the troops. Most RSMs of the older units were respected, hard, but fair, from the days when a beating in a place of a formal charge was a fair option. Done and forgotten.

I remember this RSM, Scottish, overweight ex-para with Parkinson's disease. His wife was getting laid by somebody else in the unit, no shock there, mind; his wife was fit. He was such a prick, if he hadn't been the RSM, he would have been a salesman for insurance, one of those co-op guys who used to knock on the doors of old ladies, collecting their fifty bob a week.

One night duty, in fact a Sunday night duty, I was the duty sergeant for the shift. We had two cars out, Vauxhall Cavaliers, white with an orange stripe down the sides, two-tone police horns and a blue light on the roof. Each vehicle was manned by two RMP, both armed with a 9mm Browning and a mag full of rounds, statutory police-issue handcuffs, etc. Sunday nights were notoriously quiet, so we used to allow the chaps to play snooker. The RMP snooker game was played with cars though.

The principle of the game was you would try and stop a white car, followed by a red car, then white and then another color. So, if you had a white or red car as a serviceman in the eighties in Germany, and wondered why you were stopped so often, now you know. The RMP responsible inside the duty room would keep tally of the scores. At some point during the evening, the duty sergeant would call one of the vehicles back and conduct a duty sergeant's patrol. This usually involved popping into one of the local bars, having a free Coke, compliments of the bar management, whilst enduring the scowls of other soldiers.

Our patrol was around 0230 hours, so most squaddies were at home, or somebody else's! I called Sierra 21 back to the duty room. I told the girl on duty to wait in the duty room, whilst I patrolled with the guy she was on with. His name was Joe. Red-haired, fiery temper, mad driver, all in all a good lad though.

We drove off around the 'married' quarter areas, estates that were built specifically to house soldiers and their families. It was dead, very few lights on, nobody about. We drove to a place called Hakedahl in Detmold. Again, married quarters. Some high-rise flats, others two storey, two upstairs, two down.

Joe reversed the car up against a garage. The road through the estate was one way. Therefore, four hundred yards past where we were parked was a t-junction, which took you back out onto the main public highway. We were stopped facing a hill, where the road came directly toward us down a steep hill, probably half a mile long. So, in effect, no cars could enter the estate of over five hundred families without us noticing.

We waited with windows open and...relaxed! At 0321 hours (according to the record), a set of headlights, no, two sets of headlights headed towards us. Seats up, engine on ready to stop them.

Joe said, "I'll let the first one pass and follow the second."

The first car was a small green VW Polo, it looked to be one male occupant. The number plates were German, but certainly not local. The second, again single male occupant, VW Golf GTI, white, no plates on the rear and an illegible one on the front. We pulled out behind the Golf and Joe immediately put the blue light on. To my surprise, the VW Polo sped off, and the GTI pulled over to the right just after a lamp post, on the curb.

Remember, cars in Germany were left-hand drive.

All along the road on the left were servicemen's cars, which reduced the size of the road to one single narrow carriageway, just wide enough for us to squeeze between the soldiers' cars and the now stationary Golf GTI. Joe, in the passenger seat (right side), opened his window as we drew level. The driver opened his.

Joe asked, "Hello sir, what are you doing?"

"Oh, I'm just looking around," he replied in a strong Belfast accent.

That feeling again!

Oh, fuck! Why hadn't we had our pistols on our laps?

Joe said, "I'm sorry, sir, as you are on private property, I'm going to call to get the German police to trace your car."

Immediately, the male pushed open his door, jumped out, and started to run.

Joe was like a gazelle. He caught him within fifty yards.

I was out of the car, checking the VW Golf, instantly noticing it had been hot-wired and saw the nasty looking .38 on of the floor the passenger seat. I called Joe to tell him, but he already had the guy handcuffed and was waving his 9 mm around. *Mmm,* I thought.

Now, try and picture: soldiers' cars parked all along the left side of the road; the RMP vehicle in the only remaining lane; and the Golf GTI half on the kerb on the right. So, no room for anything to pass. I recall going to the boot of the RMP car, I think to get a traffic cone to show the obstruction. As I opened the boot, I heard an engine revving from behind me.

Remember that slow-motion thing I was talking about... well, the driver of the car accelerated towards me. I thought, *wow, he wants to run me over.* Now... what were the rules governing the usage of firearms?

"Oh, fuck it!" I drew my Browning from its holster, dropped down on one knee, cocked my gun! I shouted, "Halt, police, or I'll fire!"

I remember feeling a real twat, because he obviously couldn't hear me. He was now racing towards me. I fired, double tapping through the windscreen until my mag was empty.

The Polo appeared to speed up again, but swerved before impacting into me and hit the lamp post I mentioned earlier. I ran over, pulled the car door open, dragged the driver out, and started punching him as hard as I could.

It must have been thirty seconds into the beating that Joe said, "Topper, I think he's dead."

See, it's adrenalin! I was so nervous, without realizing it, that I flipped a little. I must have hit him eight times with the shots I had fired earlier. Still suffering from confusion, I ended up frantically trying to give him CPR, until Joe said, "For fuck's sake, Topper! He's fucking dead!"

The German police arrived and took over.

The following morning about eleven, I was in bed.

Joe banged on the door. "Topper, Topper, the RSM wants you."

"Tell him to fuck off, I'm tired."

"No, no, the RSM, the OC and the RSM SIB." SIB meant Special Investigation Branch.

I reluctantly got up, dressed in something really casual, and walked over to the offices. The RSM's door was shut. I knocked.

"In," he shouted.

What a prick! I thought.

Indeed, the OC, RSM, RSM SIB, and a German civil policeman were there.

"Brown," he said in his usual self-important tone. "We have a problem."

"Really," I replied.

"The German civil police have identified the two men as members of an active service unit associated with the IRA."

"Oh, good," I said.

"Hang on," he replied. "You know nothing is ever that simple."

"What does that mean?" I asked.

"Well, how many rounds did you fire?"

"How the fuck do I know? And what does it matter now?" I said in a raised voice.

"Who do you think you're talking to?" he demanded.

"Okay, okay, let's keep it civil," the RSM of the SIB interrupted. "Topper, come down to my office, we need to chat."

I looked at the O.C, supposedly the boss. He was looking at the floor as though he knew something was wrong. No signs of support. I knew I was in the shit.

"That cunt upstairs wants to charge you for not firing single-aimed shots," said the RSM SIB.

"You're fucking joking," I replied.

"Just leave it with me for the time being. They're going to put you on OCs orders and that should just be a protocol matter (OCs orders are a military form of discipline). Just go through the motions please. I think it's for political reasons."

So no inquiry, no investigation, a good cleaning-up exercise, then they claim a pat on the back for killing a terrorist, detaining another whilst keeping absolute control of discipline. "Bollocks to that!"

"March in," screamed the RSM, as I was marched in front of the OC.

I stood to attention, staring straight into his eyes; as ever, he looked away.

"Conduct to the prejudice of good order and military discipline, contrary to Section 69 of the Army Act 1955, in that you at Hakedahl Estate on (the date) at (the time) fired a 9mm Browning, serial number _ _ _ _ , in a manner prejudicial to good order and military discipline. Are you guilty or not guilty?"

At this point I just remained silent.

The RSM screamed, "Answer the OC, guilty or not?"

I thought, *fuck them!*

"Not guilty…sir!"

The RSM was quiet now, surprise, surprise!

"Are you sure?" the OC asked.

"Yes sir, I wish to by tried by court martial."

"Well, okay, then," he said, sheepishly.

"About turn, march out," shouted the RSM, a little more compassionately though.

The RSM SIB was waiting. "Okay, Topper?" he asked.

"Yes, sir. I opted for court martial."

He burst out laughing. "Good man, good man!"

I was sent on gardening leave, which effectively means suspended for twelve weeks. I spent most of this time considering what had become of the army. Did I belong there? My dad was the epitome of a good soldier, dedicated to his country, his queen, been everywhere without moaning, but knowing he was fully supported. Yeah, bollocks. *I'm right,* I concluded.

Court martial is the most inappropriate mechanism of justice ever dreamt up in the UK. A group of old knob-heads with no experience of reality play at being judges or magistrates. They then find the youngest, most inexperienced junior officer to act as your defense lawyer. What a joke!

At 11:15 on that fateful day, I stood in front of the court martial board and answered one question.

"Do you plead guilty or not guilty?"

"Not guilty."

They babbled on for ages about the principles of the shoot-to-kill policy, the red card, military police role in Germany. God, it was boring. At lunch time, the board said they would reconvene at 1400 hours.

I sat in a small, carpeted room, trying to eat a sandwich.

The door opened and this giant of a man walked in, wearing jeans, desert boots, a green t-shirt and a black bomber jacket. He looked like a powerful guy with a placid face. "Hi, you all right?" he asked.

"Yeah, sort of," I replied.

"Personally, mate, I think you've been fucked," he said.

"And who are you then," I asked.

"I'm from the local Int cell," he replied.

I assumed at the time he meant the local intelligence unit of the intelligence corps.

"So why are you here then?" I assumed he was also in the shit.

"I think I can get you out of this," he said.

"Really," I replied, somewhat sarcastically.

"Yes, really. I'm looking for some guys to join Intelligence," he said.

Now in my naïve state of mind, I assumed Intelligence meant sitting in the 1 (BR) Corps HQ translating transcripts from East Germany, etc., which sounds quite cushy really. I assumed he had looked at my records and had found that I was fluent in German and Russian.

"How would that get me out of all this crap then," I said.

"Just leave that to me," he replied.

Wow! I thought. *What a powerful statement.*

"So, do you fancy it then?" he asked.

I was stressed to death at the time and very, very worried about the outcome of all this shit, so I said, "Yeah, go for it!" I hadn't even asked his name.

He stood up and said, "Right, then. Just wait here. I'll be back shortly."

He was only gone for twenty minutes. He burst back into the room, smiled at me and said, "Right, Topper, let's go!"

"Go where?" I asked apprehensively.

"You're finished here, case dismissed," he said.

I couldn't believe it! Little did I know. I wasn't even allowed to go back and pack; he arranged everything.

After a Land-Rover journey to another area in Germany, he introduced me to six other guys, who were equally as unprepared as I was. Facial recognition, vehicle identification, self defense, endurance....my God! What had I let myself in for? Not much information about the training, just training, training, and more training. We all spent what little free time we had speculating about what we were going to be doing. Surely this wasn't the usual Int Corp training. I'd seen Int Corp guys who would have died rather than run fifteen miles with a pack on their backs, let alone get involved in personal protection training.

This continued at a then-deemed exhaustive and ludicrous rate for eight weeks. Then on the following Monday morning, the guy that had spoken to me at the court martial met us at breakfast.

He smiled and said, "Right then, I suppose we had better start training for specifics." He went on to tell us that we would be working in Northern Ireland as part of an intelligence detachment, more commonly known nowadays as DET. I'd never actually heard of them. He discussed objectives, who we would be working with, for, and against. In conclusion, the court martial sounded like it may have been the preferred option.

After another sixteen weeks of endurance, firearms, and language training, yes, language training, we were all feeling a little more confident.

Chapter Six

For the purpose of security, I won't mention where we were based, but needless to say four weeks later, I sat in a Ford Capri with one of the other chaps, called Billy; with 9mm Brownings under our arms. We were a little confused to be working about 150 yards off the Falls Road in Belfast.

The first job was pretty easy. Two guys fitting the descriptions of those we were anticipating approached Billy in the driver's seat.

"This is the IRA. We want the car, get out!"

You've got to be fucking joking, I thought. They didn't appear to suspect who we were at all.

Billy replied, "All right," in his newly adopted East Belfast accent.

I had a magic switch on one of the gadgets issued to us, which I pressed.

The older of the men, who is now known to many people through his new political career, came around to my side. "You....out," he demanded.

As we got out of the car, a well-rehearsed exit drill resulted in both men leaning over the front of the car with no option but to stay as they were. Two minutes later, the infamous RUC blue armored landovers arrived.

We were whisked away just as the crowd started to gather.

THE NEWS

"*Two members of the provisional IRA were arrested in Belfast today. Sources say that the two men attempted to hijack a vehicle. It is believed that the occupants of the vehicle were members of the Security Services, who overpowered the suspects and handed them over to the RUC. Both men have been detained pending criminal charges.*"

"Not a bad start at all," beamed the boss. "Well done! Now go to the bar and have a celebration pint on me."

Billy and I walked from the office with smiles that would have done the good old Cheshire cat proud. We walked into the mess; well, I suppose canteen would be a more appropriate description. It had a wooden bar about four feet tall, nine stools, a few bottles of spirits placed against the wall, and hundreds of tins of beer of most types. No payment was required, hence the "Have a drink on me," from the boss.

There were about six guys at the bar, sitting on stools. They all turned and stared as we walked in.

One guy, big square chin, South African accent, about 6'4" stood up. He said, "It's the news, brothers," and started laughing.

The others joined in. We both smiled and walked over to the bar. We didn't have a clue who they were, but they seemed okay types of guys, not like usual squaddies; they were somewhat more relaxed. Anyway, they drank more than what I could manage.

I think it must have been around four in the afternoon when I was dropped onto my bunk. The following morning was all a bit vague.

We had an 11 o'clock briefing with the boss, a 1330 briefing with the RUC. We were then introduced to some of the guys we would be supporting. When I say supporting, we would provide information to control, who would evaluate its importance and credibility. If appropriate, they would ask either the RUC (in one capacity or another) or the SAS to deal with the matter. Understand 'deal' to mean whatever you want!

The general brief was to go into a specific bar on Friday afternoon about 2 o'clock, have a couple of pints, cause an argument, a fight, then get the fight to go outside. At the designated time, the cavalry would arrive and sort them out. I remember thinking that it was all a bit steep, how could you justify whacking somebody for fighting? Well, I was soon to find out.

Just after two (1400 hours), Billy and I walked into the bar; we'll call it The Falls Road Community Center. We were both dressed casually, jeans, t-shirts, etc. but nondescript, non-squaddyish. There were probably between fifteen to twenty men in the bar, no women.

It was dull, with a big Irish flag pinned to the wall directly in front as you walked in, with some Irish scribble underneath it. The bar was quite long, high, and wide. All the men in the bar were at the left side, we naturally went over to the right. Aware of the five crucial factors, we sat at the bar on stools, so as to get a complete view of the place, however, close enough to give us a clear run at the door when required. The bar fell silent for a moment as we drew ourselves up against it. It almost reminded me of that *American Werewolf in London* film, when the two Yanks walked into the Slaughtered Lamb on the moors. The look of resentment of unwanted strangers. Well, fuck 'em!

Typically British in an Irish bar.

"Two pints of Guinness, please, mate," Billy asked in a put-on cockney accent.

The barman, pale as a sheet, suggested we might wish to try the pub down the road; this was a regular's bar.

I said, "And how the fuck are we to become regulars if we can't drink here?"

He looked across at the group of silent men. One, a skinny guy with a cropped hair style, nodded his head. The barman turned his back, picked two pint glasses, and started to pour two pints of Guinness. We laughed and bartered between us for twenty minutes, having consumed three pints of Guinness. The group of guys mumbled between themselves, looking over cautiously from time to time.

Billy called the barman over and said, "If barmen pouring a pint of Murphy's can put an 'M' in the head, why don't you put a 'G' in the Guinness?"

It was just before twenty-five past two. The barman smirked and walked away.

"Oi! Knob head," Billy shouted. "I'm asking you a question!"

I remember feeling nervous. The barman continued to walk away.

"I said, I'm fucking talking to you, you prick," Billy continued.

Naturally, the bar went quiet. The skinny guy who had obviously approved our drinking turned to us and said, "Okay, lads, you've had enough, now on your way."

"And who the fuck are you? You little shit!" I replied.

"Yeah! You? Twat!" joined Billy.

Well, that about did it. Four of the larger guys came storming over, and we were away. The RV time outside was 1430 hours, so we were close enough, or so I thought. We were quite handy lads, but fuck, they were tough! We fought our way to the door, as the others stood up to join in. I remember pushing backwards against the door and falling through it. We were out...and so were the others. At the entrance to the bar, to the right, there was a small area between the buildings, used for bins and boxes.

It didn't take too long before we were losing, we were certainly overpowered. I remember praying in my mind that the backup or other team would show. I was pushed on my back and held by three, whilst Billy was being held face-down in a box. As soon as I saw him I had to laugh. Maybe it was nerves, maybe the Guinness, either way I was pissing myself, and of course, that started Billy off.

The little guy seemed none too pleased and I watched him as he took a small handgun from a holster under his trouser leg, but I still couldn't stop laughing.

"Hold the fucker still," he shouted to the three men. He tried to pull my trouser leg up, but as everybody knows, jeans don't like that, so he failed miserably. He then stood up to one side, pointed the gun at my knee and pulled the trigger. It was instantly recognizable as a 22 calibre, which is quite small. It hit my knee cap along the right leg, right side and ricocheted, hitting one of the men holding me in the upper arm.

"You fucking idiot," he screamed

The skinny guy shot at my leg again and completely missed. Just as he was contemplating his third shot, he was distracted by the screech of tires from the front of the pub. The guy holding Billy immediately let go and started running to the rear of the pub. The others let me go and walked toward the front, as if nothing had happened–too late.

CHAPTER SEVEN

THE NEWS

"Suspected members of the provisional IRA were shot dead today whilst trying to assassinate two members of the Security Forces. Members of the Security Forces were also injured during the confrontation. The RUC Chief Constable made a statement to the press..."

"These people who feel that they can assassinate, and murder members of the RUC and the Security Forces should take note. We will not tolerate this despicable and outrageous behavior. We will use all force necessary when dealing with such people."

He refused to answer questions about 'shoot-to-kill' policies and who specifically was responsible for the shootings. Back in our bar, with a few stitches, headache tablets and some gauge dressings, we were getting pissed.

We got involved in a number of such fun activities and initially, luckily, we got away without much damage. The saddest thing happened at my next call-out, best I talk about that later.

Most of us were jungle-welfare trained which I didn't really imagine was much different to working in a rain forest. We were asked for volunteers to go abroad to help train the local militia in Colombia. Usual rules though: We wouldn't really be there.

I won't go on about the basics of training as it's pretty boring. The Colombian guys were okay, if a little slow and a lot apprehensive. We had been there for approximately seven weeks and we all got called in to see Jossie.

"Right lads, you're playing Goldilocks in the forest tomorrow."

Hammer!

Pause.

"Some of the most senior drug distributors are expected at one of their factories tomorrow and you're going to take 'em out!" Nails.

"I thought we were here to train this lot to do all that shit," said Spike.

"No, you're here to do as I fucking tell you," replied Jossie, in an almost whispered response. End of that discussion then.

The following morning we set off in an inflatable around 0215 hours. We traveled for approximately thirty kilometres up river. We pulled the boat onto the bank and plotted a route to the area where these knob-heads were expected. We were looking for one of those small production plants or factories as they were more commonly known. I hated the creepy-crawlies more than anything else, and everybody knew it. Any opportunity of dropping a fucking great creepy-crawly on me, as long as it wasn't too close to the objective, was taken advantage of.

We approached our target area, which was a tin hut, a small building made of corrugated iron sheeting, with a chimney sticking out of the top. A small track led off from the entrance door down to a small boat bay by the river. The area around the hut was cleared to about fifty yards. There were six of us, so we could sleep two or make other preparations whilst the other four adopted positions in anticipation of these druggy twats arriving. Now Mr. IRA man, this is a shoot-to-kill policy!!

Around 1745 hours, a power boat came whizzing past the zone almost flat out. Three minutes later, it went back the other way, slightly slower. I mean…how fucking predictable can these people get?

On the third pass, he slowed down and pulled onto the landing area. There were four of them: one little fat guy with long curly hair, aged around forty-five to fifty; one monster of a guy who didn't look South American at all; the third, about thirty-fiveish, probably East European. The fourth was a woman.

"God," I thought, "I know what I'd like to do with her." It had obviously been a while.

She was definitely South American, about thirty, lovely, long dark hair, beautiful face. What a waste.

We let them off the boat and they wandered off into the hut. The big guy had an armalite slung over his shoulder. Smoke had been bellowing out of the chimney ever since we got there, but the hut could only have been big enough to hold four or five people. We were spread evenly apart, but in such a way that we could see each other. We had three M16 assault rifles (5.56mm American issue) and an LMG (Liaison machine gun 7.62mm, British issue). We weren't allowed a GPMG (7.62mm belt-fed British issue machine gun) because it would 'apparently' have been too obvious who we were.

I think I was 75 percent focused on whacking these lot, 5 percent wishing I could shag the fit bird and the rest worrying about creepy-crawlies.

Spike whispered, "Topper!"

"What?" I replied. We never usually had to talk.

"Look!" he pointed towards the river.

A fucking enormous snake was slithering its way up to the track from the river. It was huge. Obviously an anaconda. Now I didn't like insects, but Spike was terrified of snakes. He was also the nearest to it. As it got closer to him, I could see him slowly adjusting his position. He was obviously contemplating moving away.

I whispered, "Spike! For fuck's sake, stay where you are!"

"If it comes any closer, I'm going to shoot the fucking thing!" Amazingly, as he said it, the snake stopped. It must have been twelve feet from him. The assumption was that it had heard Spike. It reared right up. So its head must have been four feet off the floor. It sort of hovered for ages looking directly at Spike. Slowly, it then lowered its head, turned, and slid back off into the river.

"Fucking whimp!" Spike whispered, pointing towards the snake.

THE NEWS

"The newly formed local militia group shot dead five members of one of South America's drug cartels yesterday. Local people had provided intelligence enabling such an important success in the fight against drug trafficking and corruption."

Yeah, right! The following months were spent doing similar things.

CHAPTER EIGHT

Back in Northern Ireland things had heated up a lot. There was a row going on between the army and the RUC regarding control of intelligence and special ops. There was loads of shit going on regarding the chap who wrote "Fifty Dead Men Walking," and IRA grasses generally were more frequently accessible. The super grass was working!

I remember going to a briefing. At the beginning, the guy giving the brief stated quite categorically that the content of the meeting was secret and nobody needed to know anything except their own brief. This seemed unusual. The operation was called, "Knock, knock." It was the full wrath of military intelligence, special forces and RUC Special Ops, with a twist of, "Fuck it, let's get this over with!"

There were four guys per vehicle, all armed with handguns of one description or another. We used a Vauxhall Cavalier, a really old looking thing with one hell of an engine.

Our first assignment we will refer to as "Paddy." We ate early then all got together about 1850 hours. We drew our firearms and had the usual fifteen to twenty minutes reminder that if we got caught, it was our problem. We each received a photograph, address, etc., of an individual and off we went. I think everybody was particularly apprehensive. We stopped off for a pint in a bar en route, opposite the notorious Europa Hotel, cracking little place with its booths. I mentioned it earlier. You never actually knew or cared who was in as it seemed one of those places everybody went to. I remember another time I had been in there when the IRA blew up the Chinese restaurant just up the road as the RUC were known to have booked dinner there.

After a pint and a Dutch-courage Scotch, we piled back into the car, after checking it for explosives, of course. Billy verified the address, we all took one last look at the photo, and off we went again. Billy stopped the car some forty yards away from the address. We all pulled balaclavas over our faces, checked our weapons, and got out of the car.

The house was a third house in a terraced row. The curtains were all drawn, but lights were on all over the house. There was a small broken wooden fence surrounding a messy little garden with well-worn grass, so long it probably never seen a lawnmower. The wooden gate to the front door had long since rotted off. The most disturbing thing, I suppose, was one of those old kiddies' bikes, with the pedals on the front wheels, a flat metal base, and two small back wheels. An obvious indication of small children. Well, he should of thought about that.

One guy stood at the gate, one by the car, and I and a chap called Harvey, who was later to become my best pal, walked up to the front door. Harvey knocked harshly.

"Who the fuck is it?" replied a harsh female voice.

"It's the IRA, open the door," I replied in a pretty good East Belfast accent.

The woman obviously scuttled away and got her husband. The door opened and a male, aged thirty-one, 5'8", with black hair, wearing a dressing gown, stood apprehensively in front of us.

"You know why we're here," I said.

He nodded his head in acknowledgement. We were amazed, because we didn't even know why we were there.

"Wait one minute." he muttered.

I looked at Harvey, well, at his balaclava.

The guy returned within sixty seconds with a holdall.

I took it and told him to turn around.

Harvey put the pistol to the back of the man's head and pulled the trigger once. We turned immediately and walked to the car. Billy drove quietly back to where we handed over everything, including the overalls we had all been wearing. For some reason we didn't celebrate.

The following morning the brief was a bit solemn. The boss was in his usual positive mood and quickly acknowledged the low morale.

"I know it's not nice, but it's a strategy that will help us find the bastards we're looking for. Anyway, remember, that fucking holdall was being delivered to an IRA sniper, who had plans to 'do' one of our uniformed patrols last night. So, in all, you should be happy you saved some poor twat's life last night!"

The incident caused murder within the IRA; the whisperings were so loud we heard about them within twenty-four hours. It was either a renegade group who were trying to cause problems within, or the UVF; either way they never expected us.

We had quite a good relationship with the UVF, well, let's be honest, they supported British rule and agreed with us on the principle of being against a united Ireland. Whenever somebody reported an incident involving the UVF or such group, the army or RUC always managed to take prisoners.

I went to a reunion a few months ago in Belfast; it was supposed to be RUC Special Ops and a few Brit groups. I was pleasantly surprised to see so many former UVF members there, particularly those who had been released.

My father spent many, many moons over there, obviously being a para, he was one of those initially loved by everybody, then hated by the IRA and their supporters for defending themselves on that fateful Sunday. Some of the stories he told me about Armagh were fantastic except the deaths of Brits and their supporters, of course. I thought he was going to write about his experiences, but unfortunately, he died and his fabulous stories and his art of telling them died with him.

Chapter Nine

I remember the first time I met Martin McGuiness. We were doing our usual nonsense, hanging around, watching from a distance as he drove through a checkpoint. We could see him giving the squaddie a hard time, so we decided to give the squaddie a bit of a laugh. I called through and told the RMP to let him through and tell him the RUC in an unmarked car would search his vehicle just up the road. You could see his apprehension clearly and although he protested, he didn't really have much choice. Harvey drove the car across the road, thus blocking his passage. I got out.

McGuiness pulled up next to me, asking, "What the fuck is all this about?"

I replied, "Get out of the car!"

Harvey was pointing an SMG at him through the window. The RMP had the common sense to hold all other cars.

I went to the back of our car, dug an old handgun from the boot. I walked back to his window and showed him. I said, "Get out of the car, or this will be found in your boot!"

"You bastard," he mumbled as he got out.

"Now I want you to turn to the checkpoint and shout your apologies for being rude to the British soldier."

He stood and stared at me with that, "I wish I had balls!" look of his.

"Well, are we going to be a good boy?" I asked. He turned towards the checkpoint and mumbled, "I apologize."

"No," I said, "Shout it!"

He again stared at me like a good Samaritan. "I'm sorry!" he shouted.

"Oh, that's okay then, Mr. McGuiness," shouted the squaddies.

"Now, don't we feel better?" I asked.

No reply.

"You can go now," I said.

He never spoke again, simply drove off. He never even made a complaint.

Politicians my arse! He and that Adams will never be in a position to allow people to enjoy a peaceful future. Although I hate the IRA, I do believe that the Catholic community deserves a voice in a devolved government, but they should elect a politician, not a bunch of thugs. Whilst they have thugs in politics, I hope they never get a united Ireland, but I do think they are entitled to ask for it.

Anyway, it is never going to happen in my lifetime.

We got up to all sorts over there, it was good constructive fun. We thoroughly enjoyed watching the SAS whack a few and enjoyed their company when we worked together.

We, Harvey and I, booked on duty, due to drive the 2.8 litre injection Granada and with its fiddled with engine, it was a beast. We were just walking across to the car park when we received a call on the radio, something about our colleagues being involved in a chase, which was heading our way. We had worked together for two years. Nearly every day!

Usually, prior to leaving the safety of our house, we would check everything on the car, tyres, pressures, oil levels, washer fluid, brakes, etc. However, on this occasion we didn't. We both leapt into the car and away. We parked at a junction, listening to our colleagues as they approached closely following the 'bandit' car. Harvey was radio op, I was driving. He told the others to break off just prior to our junction. They did, and we were away again, chasing closely behind the car. The car was a blue Vauxhall Astra. Contrary to subsequent reports, it certainly was not joy riders.

We chased the car flat out for about fifteen minutes around housing estates up towards the hills. The driver decided to cut across a playing field, which meant coming off the road, over quite a high curb and down an embankment, in between a few trees to the sports ground. He turned probably at 60 to 65 mph and took off over an embankment. I followed. See, we were skilled drivers. Taught by the best. Regularly tested and updated. We thought we were invincible. You know that feeling you get when something is going awfully wrong, and there is nothing you can do about it? The second we took off over the embankment, the car started to twist. We must have been ten feet off the ground. On impact, into the first tree, car was almost upside down. The tree impacted almost centrally into the grill. The bonnet came through the windscreen, my seat collapsed and I disappeared into the driver's footwell. Everything stopped! Except the Vauxhall Astra.

I remember feeling something pressed against the side of my face. I remember the pain in my hips, and most importantly in my groin.

"Harvey, are you okay?" I asked.

"Not really," he replied. "I feel like my chest is collapsing."

"Don't worry, they'll be here soon," I said. "The ambulance will be here soon!"

Some three days later in hospital, I awoke. I asked could I see Harvey; the doctor kept saying, let's concentrate on you for the time being.

I had broken both of my legs, the brake pedal had embedded itself into and below my groin, the steering column had smashed my face.

Harvey was dead.

It's amazing how fragile we really are. We go through life feeling indestructible, apart from the odd accident, which most experience, broken leg, arm, wrist, etc. But everything seems to heal.

I've watched a few guys who thought, and I suppose to a certain degree, I would have agreed with, that they were indestructible. They are always the ones who are most difficult to watch die. They tend to leave us all feeling more vulnerable and fragile than we would ever usually feel.

I mean, vulnerability is an illness. It's like depression. When we feel vulnerable, we feel anxious. Anxiety is usually associated with depression. Don't ask me why, I would never profess to understanding psychiatry. Mind you, the psychiatrists that have dealt with me over the years have never understood me, so I suppose that just about explains today's psychiatry.

Harvey's death hit me pretty hard. Whilst I wasn't in the best shape myself, I knew he was dead. I struggled to maintain the ambition to carry on with life, as we didn't really have one. All the time in hospital. I spent thinking about life! I mean, what are we doing here, what's this all about, why do we live? Funny, I remember speaking to a doctor and trying to tell him how I felt. He told me it was normal to feel the way I did; it was all part of grieving. I wanted to kill him!

I was out for about eleven months. It took me a while to get fit again and even longer to accept that I would have scarred bollocks for the rest of my life. I endured the anticipated hours of doctors asking how I felt, why did I think I felt that way, and everything I felt was normal. In the end, I concluded that doctors don't know fuck about the way the mind works, but are pretty dependant on you as an individual explaining your thoughts, so they can write them in some journal and anticipate that the next guy that experiences something similar will feel the same...what shite! However, that doesn't mean I don't respect them. They did wonders fixing me up and I was so impressed with their determination. Thanks, docs!

I had a final interview with the senior psychiatrist, great guy. About 65, white hair, and those funny, half-cut glasses, which must have been a reward for doctors who were of such a high caliber and so highly paid that nothing else would satisfy their sense of achievement. Bit like a medal, I suppose. He was great, just like an actor. He sat in the same small office that I had always sat in, but with other guys. He looked across the table at me, over the top of his glasses. He was silent for about two minutes. I smiled.

He said, "So mister, how are things?"

"Fantastic," I replied.

"You mean, you're ready to leave?"

"Indeed, I am," I replied. At this point, I was unaware of the damage that been done inside my head. It's great to recover physically, but I can't quite comprehend what they mean by 'longer term effects.' Does that mean dreams, feeling insecure, paranoid, or what, specifically? The one thing I was worried about was asking what he thought was wrong. The typical behaviour of a squaddie is always to say everything's fine, even if it's not.

I received quite a welcome upon my return. The boss called me into his office and said he was sorry about what had happened to Harvey. Oh yes, Harvey. I had put him completely out of my mind.

Nevertheless, where did I want to start? I would need a few weeks of training to get back up to my fitness levels, and then I supposed it was back to sunny Belfast.

"And so you should," smiled the boss.

Little did I know the car crash had been kind to Harvey, when you consider what I would go through over the next few months!

Everything seemed calmer in Belfast. There appeared to be more people about, but looking more relaxed. The pubs we visited all seemed to be filled with happy, carefree people, a massive contrast to before. I thought for a while that it must have been me. Maybe I was seeing things through rose-tinted glasses. The bastards were here somewhere!

I arranged to meet a woman in the Lansdowne. It seemed to be the natural thing to do. Why not have some fun whilst there. The interior of the hotel is green. Nice place, but obviously supporters of the other side. You enter the hotel via the car park, which is just to the side of the building. You go through the green reception area, to the left of the stairs. On the left is a glass door, with both a bar and coffee or food area inside. Up the stairs were the hotel rooms.

I walked into the bar area. Nobody seemed in any way interested. I approached the bar, which was virtually surrounded by people, all dressed as though they were going somewhere more disco-ie after here. I supposed this was a great place to start before going into Belfast for a nightclub. I felt relaxed and smiled at the bar girl as she approached me.

"I'll have a large brandy, please," I asked politely.

"You want Coke and ice with that," she replied.

"No, thanks," I said.

Again, nobody showed any interest. I settled down on a bar stool, and when my drink arrived, I paid and thanked the girl. I looked around the area. It was nice, very relaxed, nobody sitting in corners looking sheepish, nobody looking confrontational. No, it was really nice. It was around seven forty-five. I was a bit early. We had arranged to meet at eight. Good opportunity for me to suss the place out. There was a woman sitting to my left who looked like she was waiting for somebody. She kept looking at her watch, then looking around the room. She had that agitated look of 'wait till that tosser gets here' about her. Her date was obviously late.

There was a bunch of civil-looking guys to my right, all laughing and joking. Talking about each other's wives and girlfriends. The old 'your wife makes an awful breakfast' joke being bantered about, and 'I thought it was your mother, not your wife' comments. All in jest of course, hence all the laughing. One of them caught me looking and obviously listening. I smiled and looked away.

"Hey, you all right?" he asked.

I chose to ignore him.

He walked the yard across to my stool and again asked, "You all right??

"Fine, thanks," I replied.

"Waiting for your girl?" he asked.

"Yes, late as ever," I lied, starting to feel a little uncomfortable.

"Want to join us?" he asked, staring straight into my eyes.

"No, but thanks anyway."

"Where you from, you have a funny accent."

Oh, fuck, was my next thought. I really didn't want to get involved in a conversation with this guy. He was obviously pissed and starting to get a little overconfident with me. In my usual charming way, I said, "I told you I don't want to drink with you. I told you I was waiting for my girl. Now fuck off and leave me alone!" And I smiled.

"For fuck sake, Eric, leave the man alone," squawked one of his friends.

I turned my stool around slightly, and ended up facing the girl.

"Ignore him, he's a drunk," she said. She must have been thirtyish, black hair, slim, very pretty. I remember wishing she was the girl I was supposed to be meeting.

"No harm done," I said.

"I overheard you say you were waiting for your girl. Is she late?" she asked in a broad Belfast accent.

"The truth is, I don't think she's coming now. I think you call it being stood up!" It seemed funny rather than embarrassing. Strange that.

CHAPTER TEN

I know in my younger days, like at school, and a few years thereafter, I was particularly shy when it came to good-looking girls. Don't get me wrong, I had been with more than my fair share, but all for sex, no real intentions of a relationship.

We had some really weird situations with girls when we were kids. I think it was something to do with the close environment, being soldiers kids that is. Also, growing up in places like Germany, where pornography was legal, we were used to finding porn films and mags all over the place. Well, I suppose then, as young boys, the fantasy was to act out what we had seen.

Some of the guys involved will remember a specific incident in a church yard in our small German town called Lippstadt. I know the parents still alive of those of us involved will be surprised to hear this, but we had watched an 8mm cine film of four guys having sex with one woman in a church yard in the dark. Alan and Vince (brothers), Mike and I, all arranged to meet in our local church yard about 8 pm on one Friday night.

Alan said he had arranged with one of our local girls for her to come along, but, as per the script, she would arrive about twenty minutes after us. I never really had any fear of graves; I was always of the opinion that those buried there had gone, hopefully to heaven.

It was early summer, so it was warm, and still quite light. We arranged ourselves around an area full of large crypts, or the rich dead area, we used to call it. Vince, Mike and I lay hidden behind three crypts. Alan lay on a grassy area in the open. We weren't worried about anybody coming along as we had walked through this place many a night before and never been confronted by anybody.

Smack on time, she arrived. Annette, gorgeous girl, well developed and very much up for the game. She was fourteen; so were we!

She had an all-in-one corduroy cat suit on, which zipped all the way from the crotch to the neck. She walked across to Alan, who was leaning on one arm on the floor. They spoke for a few seconds and she immediately removed her shoes and lay on the ground beside him.

It was so exciting, but at the same time scary.

He leant over and started kissing her. He pushed her gently backwards so she was lying flat on the grass. We were all silent, but I'm sure thinking along the same lines. He fumbled for her zip, around her neck, still kissing her. He pulled the zip down, all the way down. He stopped kissing her and stood up. Clutching both of her hands he pulled her to her feet. By this time, we could all see that she had very little if anything on under the cat suit.

He continued kissing her and pushed the shoulders of the cat suit over her back, revealing her naked torso and her ever so pert breasts. He pulled her toward him, and pushed the suit down over her buttocks and down to her feet. She stepped out of it...naked! I remember thinking how well developed she was. She had full breasts, perfect curves and a well groomed target area, she was a real woman. Well for us at the time she was. This was consenting sex between five underage people. I had considered that before. I had seen a thing on the telly where men had raped a woman; she had screamed and said no. This wasn't like that, in fact I later learnt from her that she had loved it and wanted it as much, if not more, than us. That was during a conversation nearly six years later...whilst doing a bit of reliving the past (sorry to her then-husband, nothing personal!).

Well, I wasn't sure if we were to join in or not, but regardless, I was so excited, it was better than any film or mag.

They both lay back down on the grass, again kissing and rubbing each other all over. He pushed her legs apart with his knees and was quickly up against her, with his obvious excitement. Mike suddenly jumped up and walked over. She wasn't surprised to see him. So I got up as well. She looked at me and smiled. Vince quickly followed. Alan thrust inside her...she groaned. It was so exciting; we were fourteen.

She put her arm out and was reaching over to Mike. He moved forward slowly. She grasped toward his trousers. He very quickly undid his belt and got them off. He didn't need any arousing. He leant over and she took him into her hand. She began masturbating him slowly, whilst Alan by this time was thrusting frantically. She looked over at me and said, "Come on, we aren't staying all night."

I took off my trousers and undies and moved over toward her. She beckoned me closer until I was right next to her face. Then she did the unbelievable; she pulled me by my penis and started sucking...well, this was my first ever blow job, and in such circumstances...

Alan jumped up and obviously couldn't wait any longer. It went everywhere, all up her stomach as he pulled away. It went onto Vince's trousers, but she still didn't stop sucking. I was in heaven.

Mike had been waiting his turn…I won't say patiently, but been helping himself along a little.

Alan stood up and said to Mike, "Remember to pull out."

Mike didn't seem to listen, he was inside her like a ferret.

I felt myself explode into her mouth, that uncontrollable feeling that all men can't resist. My body pumped and she swallowed; at the same time Vince came all over the side of her head. Fuck, there was sperm everywhere. Mike had only been inside her for a few seconds and started jerking around all strangely. I looked at her...she smiled. I stood up and I remember my face feeling flushed and I felt really guilty. Not that she hadn't willingly participated, but at the crudeness of the whole scenario.

And then she shouted, "what the fuck are you doing?"

We looked at her in panic! Was this the point that she had changed her mind? Surely not! No.

Oh shit, Mike had come inside her! He had broken the golden rule…the only rule. In those days things like AIDs and things were never heard of. The big thing was single parent pregnancies.

Mike got up and sheepishly mumbled, "Sorry."

I remember months later her dad knocking on people's doors and accusing every Tom, Dick, and Harry. She left school shortly after, never to be seen again...well, for some years anyway. Funny thing in those days, being a soldier's child.

Chapter Eleven

"Well, looks as though we are both in the same situation," the Irish girl at the bar said, smiling as though it was a good thing.

"Best I buy you a drink then," I replied.

"Best you do," she replied in a somewhat sexy manner.

My, I thought, *this really is going to be my lucky night.*

It must have been around midnight when she followed me up the stairs into my hotel room. I let her in and told her I was going to the toilet. The room was small, but big enough for a tidy double bed, a chest of drawers, and a lot of mirrors.

The separate toilet gave me the opportunity of to hide my 9mm. A small, convenient, little airing cupboard with towels and stuff in it was ideal. I pushed it up against the wall, and turned the end of the bottom towel against the wall, so I could also see if she had found it. I splashed a little water around the sink, flushed the toilet and went back into the bedroom.

"Thought this was the good old days, did you?" snarled the guy who had confronted me at the bar.

The girl stood at the door looking a little embarrassed, his other two mates were stood either side of the bed. For a moment I considered running back into the bathroom and retrieving my 9 mil, but by the time I had it they would not only have caught me, then also had the gun…shit!

"Oh, don't tell me this is your wife?" I exclaimed.

"Oh no, no, no, this is the wife of one of our brave comrades who is spending time in the kesh thanks to you, you Brit bastard," he replied viciously.

"I don't know what you're talking about," I said, realizing this wasn't quite what I expected.

The man was vicious; you could see it in his eyes. Not one of the older hats with their old fashioned methodologies, this was a real spiteful prick. The other two kept quiet. Both stared at me without saying a word.

"Turn around and put your hands behind your back," he insisted.

I did as he asked. I could feel the plasticcuffs being tightened, almost cutting the blood supply completely. I started to feel very apprehensive.

"Go check the toilet," he bawled to the larger one of his colleagues. "I'll bet he's stashed a gun in there." He stood silent whilst the man searched the bathroom, constantly staring at me. Weird, you get those people who can stare for ages without blinking and the likes of me that, if I try, I get tears in my eyes. Not that I intended having a staring match with this guy. He didn't have to wait for long for an excuse to lose his temper a little more though.

"Lookie here," said the guy as he walked from the toilet with my 9 mil.

"That's not mine," I smirked. As I turned to look at Mr. Nasty, I felt a thud on the back of my head.

I woke, God only knows how much later. I felt awful. I was naked, I knew that and a Hessian sack was covering my head. My hands were still tied behind my back and my head was throbbing.

It was quiet, but warm. I wondered for a minute if I was still at the hotel. Nah, they weren't that stupid, someone would have seen me come in and at least my reliable date may have noted my absence at some point.

"He's awake," said a deep voice, with a really coarse southern Irish accent.

I felt as though the room was enormous, although I couldn't obviously know. It was as though we were in a lecture arena, or maybe it was just the way I felt because I was naked.

"Just think to yourself for a minute, boys. If we had been a little later, that horrible Brit prick would have been fucking one of our heroes' wives. Doesn't that make you sick?"

There were grumbles of agreement; I think there were three others in the room. He certainly wasn't the guy from the hotel room.

I suppose the most difficult thing in circumstances like these is to think of any way out. If you do or say the wrong thing, then not only will the anticipated beatings get worse, but the inevitable death will probably be more prolonged. I find the best bet is to agree with everything they say, in their words, not your own, and act as though you're past caring.

Within a few minutes, the fun started. I think it must have been a cane of some description. It's worse that you can hear and not see, because you can't brace yourself quickly enough. You can hear that whoosh sound as it comes through the air, but can't exactly tell where it's going to impact. The feet! For fuck's sake…the fucking feet. It felt like someone had placed a red hot iron on my feet...

I screamed. One of my big problems has always been anger management. Although I convince myself that I can always play cool, scared, in control, when I get hurt I have this horrendous temper, probably a bit like the prick playing with my feet. Before I could catch my breath, he struck me again and again and again.

"I'm going to fucking burn you when I get hold of you, you Irish wanker," I screamed. Probably not one of my cleverer moments.

"Oh, fucking really!" he screamed. He moved the blows around a bit more, onto my arms, my stomach, my shins. It was agony.

It's an awful sensation when someone is doing something so painful to you and there is nothing you can do to stop it. He doesn't really want anything from you and there isn't much you could give him to make him stop. It's just the sheer pleasure of a brutal maniac finally being permitted to fulfill his sick fantasy.

It must have gone on for about twenty minutes. I was exhausted. Everything stung rather than hurt. He went quiet. I heard a couple of them giggling. Always a bit concerning.

Then I could smell something weird. Vinegar, I could smell vinegar. Of course, the cane would have cut through my skin. The vinegar was a very logical move. I only felt it being tipped over my thighs, then I passed out. The good thing about being in the army in such circumstances, you will always be missed. If you're not where you're supposed to be at a specific time, you will be missed, and the beauty of being in Ireland, everyone will always work the reverse of the police. They will always think the worst.

Unbeknown to me at the time, just about everyone was out looking for me. Not that it would help for the next three days though.

Chapter Twelve

When I woke up, I was still stinging all over. Not only could I smell vinegar, but they or he had obviously urinated over me, another form of acid I suppose, but an obvious sign of frenzy. I was surprised that only one person spoke ever. This obviously wasn't an IRA punishment squad. Punishment squads were far more professional, brutal, but to the point…almost soldiers…well, almost.

"He's awake again," mumbled a slightly spoken man, with an obvious Belfast accent. He sounded very young.

"Shall I get the boys from the unit?" he asked.

"No, I haven't finished yet," demanded the guy with the harsh southern Irish accent.

"Are you enjoying yourself as much as we are, Brit?" he said.

Assuming the question was directed at me, I replied, "You mean, you are enjoying yourself. Seems to me you're alone, you prick!" Again, maybe not another of my best choice of words.

Now this time, it certainly was not a cane. The first strike against my right leg broke it instantly. Fuck, that hurt. Both my fib and tib snapped straight through. Believe it or not, that was a positive thing. I was in so much pain, the rest didn't really matter.

I remember him finding the scars on my balls.

He was quite funny about it, really! "My we have had a rough ride in the past, haven't we, Brit?"

Then, ever so slowly and gently, whilst having me held down, he started re-cutting them open with what felt like a razor blade.

Believe it or not, by that time I didn't care. I thought I would die at some point. I remember dreaming quite a bit. About my childhood, about my early days in the army. How easy everything had been, how simple life should be. It must have been early on the fourth day, I was woken by someone throwing a freezing bucket of water over me. I vaguely remember two or three people arguing. One quite specifically stated that "we are the fucking IRA, you call US if you think you have a BRIT! What the fuck have you done to him, for fuck's sake?" Whoever he was, he wasn't very happy.

The same guy leant over to me and said, "I don't know who you are, but this isn't the way. No matter what you have done, this isn't the way!"

I know now what he meant, but I didn't then. I was wrapped in blankets and carried into some kind of vehicle. There was a lot of arguing and shouting going on. I heard a gun shot and imagined it was me being shot, but it obviously wasn't. Whoever was moving me obviously was angry with what had gone on. Surely this wasn't the IRA saving me from some dissident group.

I was dropped off (literally), just outside Belfast city center. Still wrapped in blankets, I was in so much pain, I didn't want to move, but the taste of fresh air was fantastic. Someone gently pulled the blanket from my face. That was the first time I realized that the sack had been removed from over my head. It was obviously a woman; no man could replicate that scream.

I spent a year in hospital being operated on, again playing shrink games and generally feeling as though I wasn't really there at all. *Maybe I had died,* I often thought to myself.

One thing is for sure; my poor bollocks would never be the same again.

After twelve months, I was again transferred to the psychiatric wing at Woolwich military hospital. I remember sitting in front of the same psychiatrist and having a very similar discussion, but this time the outcome would be different. It was over, it was time to leave.

Me, a civilian. What? How on earth would I cope? I was transferred to the Military Police Post in Aldershot to finalize my last details. I think a story was concocted to put everybody at ease. I was told that everybody had been informed I had transferred from Germany after being involved in an accident. It was awful. I was still depressed. I was attached to the quartermaster's store, where I worked for a great guy. He found me one day sitting in a car crying. He took me inside and made me a cup of tea.

I know he later went to see the RSM, who insisted that I be seen by the local psychiatrist. As per the book, I didn't tell him anything. So he transferred me to Woolwich. Round and round we go again! I stayed there, under supervision for a few months. Then I was left to go my own way.

Funny, the army. Always want the best out of you, expect you to give your best. Indoctrinate you to believe that the army is your family, then when you're spent, finished, and had enough; they discard you like a used sanitary towel. Not just me, I must say. Any other business would be dragged in front of the court and instead, upon that, they look after their cast-offs, but not the army! I knew the rest of my life would be a lie, I knew I would struggle to attain normalility, but then, as per usual, you don't have a choice. Survive or lose!

Chapter Thirteen

I got a train from Aldershot into London. From there I got a train to Reading. Someone had told me I could get a job working in security. Security, hmm, that must be similar to what I was used to, maybe a little downgraded, but similar…surely. Well, fuck me. I had never seen such a shower of shit in all my life. They called this the civilian security industry, what a load of bollocks. The organizations were run by people with no security experience, regulations written by the people who were least likely to abide by them, or have to, and governed by people who didn't really care. Nice! No wonder crime was such a winner in the UK.

I went to see this company, rang the bell.

A man answered. "Hello, R Security. Can I help you?"

"Yes, I was told you are recruiting security staff."

"Oh, yes come in."

Good start.

I sat in the reception for about twenty minutes until a middle-aged man came across to me and said, "You looking for a job?"

"I am indeed," I responded.

"When are you available to start?" he asked.

"I've just got to sort out somewhere to stay and then I'm all yours," I replied.

The man escorted me into his office and picked up the telephone. He sorted out a job, a house for me to stay, and even arranged for someone to take my gear to the house.

"Right, then, mate, just fill in this form and you can start tonight at seven."

I was gob smacked. I had not long since walked into this place, I was walking out with somewhere to stay and a job…wow. He didn't even know my name. I filled in the form with some bullshit detail and he escorted me to the door. Outside stood this enormous white Rhodesian guy.

"Right, mate, I'll look after you from here."

He drove me to a two-story house. On the way, he asked me where I was from. I told him I had been in the military police for some years, and had decided it was time to find my feet in the real world.

I worked as a security guard for nearly one hundred hours in the first week; I didn't even know how much they were paying me. I remember every time I finished a shift, the guy would call me and ask me to do another shift as someone had let him down. I suppose I was a little naïve. It varied from hospital reception areas to industrial sites.

The house I was staying was more like a squat than anything else. There were about five of us. They all seemed ill-disciplined and lazy, but to be fair I was just out of the army and probably could never imagine myself being any other way than self-disciplined. I never really made the effort to get to know any of them, not that any of us had the time. We were either asleep or being asked to cover shifts of those that never turned up. What chaos, this wasn't security, it was slave labor.

I was asked to work in a building next to the Reading festival, purely to stop people getting in to use the toilets and crash out. Easy enough. Nobody really tried. After the second day, a woman, probably in her early thirties, knocked on the door. The building was one of those new glass-fronted things, so unless you were in the toilet or shower everyone could see you. She looked decent enough. I unlocked the door.

"Yes, Madam, what can I do for you?" I asked politely.

She explained that she had a burger stall out front and would be there for around thirty-six hours. There would only be her and her sister, so if they had any problems, could they call me. Well, I wasn't sure what the protocol in the situation was, so I just agreed.

"You're a love," she said as she walked off.

I watched with interest as she and her sister parked this thing in front of my building, lifted the front, got their bib things on and started their grill. It seemed quite professional. People started to turn up and their little scheme seemed to be doing well. After a couple of hours, the sister walked over and knocked on the door.

I opened it and asked, "Are you okay?"

"Yes, just wondered if I could use the loo," she asked. I couldn't figure out the accent, it was a sort of cockney, come West Country mix. Nice though.

I let her in.

"Oh, I'm Sue and my sister is Marlene," she explained.

"Hi I'm..." *Fuck, what do I say?* This was a first. "Sorry, I'm Tom."

She looked at me, all confused, and shrugged her shoulders. I showed her to the toilet; it was at the rear of the building. She went in. I waited.

"You out there?" she shouted.

"Yes, sorry, do you want me to leave?" I replied.

"No, no, I just wondered, where are you from?" she asked.

"Liverpool," I replied.

"You haven't got a scouse accent though, have you?" she shouted through the door.

"No, I grew up abroad. My old man was in the army," I replied.

"That must have been exiting," she said.

I got this funny smell waft past me all of a sudden. It smelt awful.

"You okay in there?" I asked.

"Yes, sorry, I'm just finishing a spliff I started this morning."

Well, fuck me, I hadn't been out of the army five minutes and I was surrounded by druggies and hippies.

"You trying to get me in trouble?" I asked.

She opened the door, it smelt like a doss hole. She was pretty, obviously the younger of the two. Long dark hair, white, semi-open top on, showing her cleavage, tight jeans. "Take it you have been away for a while and this job is just filling time for you," she said, looking at me inquisitively

"What makes you say that?" I asked.

"Because everybody smokes dope nowadays. It isn't such a big issue anymore," she informed me.

I must admit she didn't look worried at all. It was as though she was smoking a normal cigarette. I remember once trying a 'spliff' whilst in the army, when I was around seventeen, in Germany. We were with twenty-three Bty, twenty-seven Field Regiment, based in Lippstadt. Probably the most enjoyable non-pressured time in my life, around the time I referred to when I first joined, when Terry Farrow was waiting for me as I returned from my birds.

Anyway, I remember a guy called Pete Cartwright, God knows what he was doing in the army; he certainly wasn't into rules and regulations. He was well into the whacky-backy though. Those were the days when smoking dope, etc., whilst almost undetectable (unless you were stoned!), was much forbidden in the services. He was known as one of the guys who regularly smoked it, regardless. One night, probably about eleven, he was playing his weird music really loud. I went and banged on his door to ask if he would turn it down. He eventually opened the door and whilst he was there in person, I couldn't promise that he was not there in mind. Shame, really, he was a good guy when not stoned. He opened the door and it really was like a case of lights on, no one home.

"Do us a favor, Pete, turn the music down a bit," I asked politely.

"Want a drink?" he replied.

Well, I was awake anyway. Not being much of a drinker, I was quite shocked when he poured me bourbon. Not just because it was straight, but also because I had never tried it before. After a few glasses, he started smoking one of his special cigarettes. He offered it to me.

"No, thanks, mate. I'll give it a miss," I declined.

A little later and a few more bourbons, I tried it.

I'll have to skip to the next morning, as the rest of the night was a blur. I remember standing on parade. We used to wear green overalls, a green plastic belt around our waists, and boots and puttees. I don't know who, but I had someone hold me by my belt to ensure I could stand up, and once parade was over, I was hidden in the camouflage net store until half four that afternoon.

So naturally, I blamed the sickness on the funny cigarette, not the bourbon, thus I never touched it again.

"Want to try it?" Sue asked me.

"Ah, no, thanks, I've tried it before. It just made me ill."

"It also makes you horny," she replied.

I was scared shitless. You see, the thing with forward men, they are always dead self confident. So when a woman reverses the role, they…me included, shit themselves. I think I just smiled, whilst she seemed to be staring at me.

"Suppose I'd best get back to serving burgers before my sister gets worried," she finally said.

I let her back out of the front door. There didn't appear to be too many people standing in the queue anymore, which was a good indicator that the festival was about to get under way. I put the door on the latch and went outside for some fresh air.

Just as I got outside, Marlene popped her head out of the door to the burger bar.

"Fancy a burger, Tom?" she asked.

"Yes, go on then, why not. But don't put loads of stuff on it. I'd rather just have the burger and the roll please," I replied.

A few minutes later, she delivered, exactly how I had expected it. She wasn't too bad looking either, but she had really weird-colored hair. Well, it seemed it to me at the time. It was black with like dark red stripes in it.

"I like your hair," I lied.

"Really. Strange, most men hate it. They say I'm an exhibitionist," she replied.

"Listen," she said, looking me straight in the eye. "Would you let me and my sister stay in the building overnight? It wouldn't half help. See, we have to stay here, otherwise we could lose our pitch overnight, and the punters start coming over for breakfast buns about five in the morning," she said.

"To be honest, I should be changing shift at seven, in about half an hour, so you'll have to ask the night man. If it were me, I'm sure we could sort something out."

At ten past seven, as per usual, the phone in the building rang.

"Security," I answered.

"Hi, mate. It's to control room. We haven't been able to sort your replacement. Would you mind staying on until the morning? The duty manager says he will pay you double time, and make sure you're relieved in the morning. He said he isn't bothered if you just lock yourself in and sleep. You only have to do check calls every three hours instead of hourly."

Fucking typical, I thought to myself. But well, what else would I be doing, apart from sleeping in the doss house, waiting to find where I was in the morning? At least this was clean and I could listen to the music from the festival until late. And free food all night.

I went outside after pretending to be dead offended on the phone.

Marlene came over again, carrying a plastic cup of coffee. "Here you go. Looks like your relief is late then."

"I won't be getting relieved. They have cocked up the shift pattern again," I explained.

"Oh well, looks like you'll have to put up with us for the night," she said.

I looked at her; she winked and walked off back to the burger bar.

It was a lovely warm evening, so I picked up one of those leather reclining office chairs and put it outside the building where the sun was shining. I took off my company issue tie, undid my top buttons, put a box under my feet, and lay back and relaxed. If they weren't really bothered or concerned, why should I be?

It was quite nice really, although I didn't really like the music much. It was good to just sit outside and watch the world go by. After an hour, I noticed that there weren't any punters at the burger bar, but I could hear the girls laughing and giggling. Weird, these non-military people.

I must have fallen asleep, probably been out for about another hour. Someone was shaking me. It was quarter to ten. The sun had gone in and the temperature was dropping.

It was Sue. "Thought I'd better wake you. It will be freezing out here shortly," she explained.

"Thanks. God, I must have been miles away," I said.

"You were. We haven't had any punters for about an hour and a half, but we have been amused by watching you wriggle around in your chair." She giggled.

I felt a bit embarrassed.

"Anyway, would it be okay if we stayed in the building? Promise we won't be any hassle, and won't smoke in there," she asked, with a big beaming smile.

"Why not? I don't think I'll be getting any visitors tonight anyway."

She skipped back to their van, and obviously informed her sister of the good news.

"Sue," I shouted.

She came back out of the van.

"What time do you finish there, as I'll have to let you in?" I asked.

"We should be done in about half an hour, if that's okay," she replied.

They seemed okay to me. Apart from the little dope smoking excursion, they had been quite nice and friendly.

On the dot, half an hour later, there was a knock on the door. I was semi-awake.

I opened the door, and they both stood there, carrying blue sleeping bags.

"Fully equipped then?" I asked innocently.

"Let's hope you are," replied Marlene, as they walked in.

Hmmm. Wasn't quite sure if I should answer that, so I didn't.

Sue was explaining that they were both dancers, but her husband had left her about a year ago, and always used to bring his burger bar to the festival. He made a fortune. So as he had left it behind, they had decided that they would take the opportunity. It was a break from work, and they got to meet loads of people with their clothes on...

Stupidly, I asked, "With your clothes on?"

"Yes, we're exotic dancers, so most of the time we dance at rich guys' private parties, which usually ends with everybody naked." Sue smiled.

I could feel myself blushing.

"Don't be embarrassed, we're not hookers or anything."

I suppose to me, they were the same as. All the bars we had been to throughout the world, you could usually get a shag out of the dancers. But then again, I suppose I had never really lived in England.

"Marlene used to do massage and all that, but it got a bit spooky going into people's houses on your own and never really knowing who you were dealing with."

They went on for ages, talking about their business experiences, ex-husbands, fetishes, futures. They were interesting. Unusual but interesting.

I had started to feel weird over the past few days; I wasn't sure what it was, so like every good member of the male population, I decided to ignore it. When I did sleep, I had started dreaming. Strange dreams, all violent or sad. Maybe it was just a change thing that people go through.

Sue was lying back on her sleeping bag, Marlene was lying on her front, kicking her legs up behind her. I still sat in my comfy swivel chair. Sue suddenly changed all conversation and said, "Think it's time I got changed."

"Changed into what?" I asked.

"My PJs. I can't sleep in jeans, they cut off the circulation."

"Me, too," grinned Marlene.

"Nice to have a choice," I added.

They both smiled.

"Is there a shower in here," asked Sue.

"Yes, it's the room next to the toilet you used earlier," I told her.

They both got up, grabbed a holdall, which they must have been sharing, and wandered off in the direction of the shower. I had the usual male rude thoughts about the two of them in the shower.

I called the control room and told them everything was okay. The duty controller told me I might as well get my head down, he wouldn't phone me unless it was urgent, and he sympathized with the fact that I was doing back-to-back shifts.

I walked down the small corridor to the toilet. I could hear the shower running, as I grabbed the toilet door handle. I pushed the door open.

"Oh sorry!" I exclaimed when I noticed Marlene sitting naked on the toilet.

"It's okay," she laughed. "I should have locked the door."

I felt a right Pratt. I heard the toilet flush and I stood slightly away with my back turned as I heard the door open.

"Okay, Tom. It's free now."

"Sorry," I repeated. I turned around and she still stood there naked. She smiled.

"You're shy!" she said.

"I'm not; I just don't want you to think you owe me anything for staying in here," I said.

She walked over to me. She was pretty, her body was very firm; and I was struggling to keep my eyes above her chin level. By now she was about six inches away from my face. She leant forward, put her right hand behind my head, and pulled my lips onto hers. We kissed for a couple of seconds, tongues; breathing quite heavily...well, I was anyway.

She pulled away gently, and said, "Better go and have my shower."

Have you ever tried to piss with an erection? It's a real pain in the arse. You have to stand four feet away from the toilet and piss into the air; getting the elevation, bearing, and trajectory right is nigh on impossible.

I wiped the missed bits off the floor, washed my hands, flushed the toilet, and returned to my chair.

Sue came along the corridor and suggested making a coffee. She had a white nighty on; it didn't leave much to the imagination.

"I'm okay, thanks," I said.

She lay down on her sleeping bag with her legs toward me. She lay flat with her hands behind her head, didn't say anything, just stared at the ceiling. Funny, it didn't feel like an uncomfortable silence. "Have you got a sleeping bag?" she asked.

"No, I didn't think I was here for the night," I replied.

"Well, I could spread mine across the floor; we could use Marlene's as an over cover, and we could all share. If you want to of course," she offered.

"That's very kind of you," I said, feeling all aroused all of a sudden.

She arranged the bags. I went to great lengths to explain that I didn't have any pyjamas or anything.

"Tom, it's fine; we won't bite you."

Marlene returned looking all flushed; she had a pair of white satin shorts on and a white, see-through top.

"Well this looks cozy," she said.

"Tom hasn't got a sleeping bag," Sue explained.

"Good," Marlene replied.

They both got under the sleeping bag, and we carried on, talking shit for about ten minutes. I got up and started to undress. There was a noted silence. I was still badly scarred.

"Fuck's sake," semi-shrieked Marlene.

"What are those scars from?"

"Oh, old army injuries," I explained.

"What happened?" asked Sue.

"I'd rather not discuss it, if you don't mind."

"No, that's fine. Get in here and let us have a closer look."

Riot Control
"Londenderry Northern Ireland"
1975

25 pounder live firing artillery exercise
1979

"Bullshit Baffles Brains!"
1977

"First parachute jump."
1978

"Now That's What You Call A Parachute!"

"Spot the wellies, tends to put snakes off."

"6 weeks in the jungle"

"The Aftermath of an IRA Bomb"
1986

"Fully air conditioned"
Over 1000 rounds of ammunition used

"Mult-Para Descent into the Desert"
1991

Most of the scars would eventually disappear...apart from the ones I really wanted to. Like my bollocks. After a few minutes of them admiring my war wounds, we were all kissing. It was quite spooky. I was paranoid about coming straight away and kept stopping for a breath, trying to think of other things, anything but the current situation, hoping it would make me last a bit longer. It was great, inside one, then the other; whilst one was kissing me, the other was all over me, kissing, kicking, sucking. Think I could like this job.

I woke about seven. There was a banging on the door. The girls had gone.

I opened the door to be greeted by a policeman.

"Hi there, are you okay," he asked.

"Yes, why, what's wrong?" I asked.

There were police cars all over the place; the whole area was taped off.

"Have you been here all night?" he asked.

"Yes, why, what's happened?" I asked again.

"There's been a dreadful accident. Two young women have been burnt to death in the burger van over there. They must have slept in it and not turned everything off properly. I'll give you chance to get sorted out and I'll have to get a statement off you. Did you see anything?"

I was dumbstruck to say the least; I genuinely didn't know what the fuck was going on. I stood staring at the police guy.

"Are you okay?" he asked again.

"Yes, I'm just surprised. I met them yesterday. They gave me a free cup of tea and a burger."

"I'm sorry. It's dreadful I know, but I'll come back in an hour and get a statement," he repeated.

On the following Monday, I went to the office. I requested a transfer to Liverpool, as it was nearer home. The boss explained that they don't usually do transfers as each branch stands on its own, but he would phone and find out. I also told him I needed a couple of days off to go home. He agreed.

Chapter Fourteen

I got my transfer, to Warrington in Cheshire, it was the closest office. It was horrible. I only wanted to work nights. I couldn't sleep anyway, so it would do me a favor. I worked all over the place again. They would ship people from Manchester to work in Liverpool and vice versa. How they made any money was beyond me. Wasn't my problem though, I suppose.

I had just finished a shift in Manchester and rarely had the following night off, so on the way back, I stopped off in Warrington and went for a drink. That was a new experience. Although I had been out near my parents' house a couple of times, I had never really been out on my own amongst complete strangers in a pub.

It was a grubby place, opposite the railway station in Warrington. The police station was on the back of it, so it was typically a copper's pub. The bar was long, but cozy. There must have been between fifteen to twenty people inside. Some sat down, others sat at the bar. As I walked to the bar, everybody seemed to be staring…or I was paranoid.

The bar lady was young, probably twenty-two to twenty-five blonde, an obvious smoker, but pleasant enough.

"Hello, love. What can I get you?"

"Just a pint, please," I replied.

"Of?" she asked.

"Sorry. Guinness, please," I said, feeling a little stupid.

She poured and, smiling, put the pint in front of me.

"Take it you're not from round here then?" she asked, making polite conversation.

"Why?" I answered almost instinctively.

"No reason, just trying to make conversation," she said, screwing her forehead as though offended.

"Listen, I'm sorry. I've had the day from hell," I said, feeling like a right idiot.

"It's okay, love, we all have them. I'll leave you to your pint."

I sat on the stool, looking all over the bar. It felt strange; I couldn't imagine anybody in there being IRA or army. Let's be honest, you can never confuse a copper with a squaddie.

I ordered another.

"Hi, Reachard," squealed a voice from the doorway.

It was Rachael from the office. She was the administration manager or something. She seemed nice enough, ugly as sin, mind, but nice. "I didn't know you drank here," she said.

"I don't normally; I just thought I'd have a couple on the way home from work, as I'm off tomorrow."

And then it happened, I had my first ever mind flash as I like to call it. I had this sudden vision of holding a small dog up in the air by its collar and slowly strangling it to death and I remember feeling a kind of rush through my arms, making me grit my teeth.

"You okay?" she asked.

"He's having a bad day," the bargirl said, butting in.

"Yes, sorry. You just reminded me of someone," I lied. "Want a drink?" I asked her, trying to cover my thoughts.

"Yes, gin and tonic with ice, please," she said, still staring at me.

We sat and chatted for an hour or so. She was intrigued as to why I was working as a security guard. She had obviously seen that I had been in the army, but my records gave no indication of what I really had been up to.

In fact, when you leave the army, you used to be given a little red book. For all your efforts in those days, your release was recorded as a paragraph in Queen's Regulations, and they would write a few words about you. Now considering that your future was based on it, you would expect it to be perfect. Well, according to mine, I am 5'6" tall, have blue eyes and blond hair and my last posting was Canada. It wouldn't have been so bad had they at least discussed that with me. I'm 6' tall, have brown eyes and brown hair. My record states that I was an asset to the Military Police and that I could work unsupervised. No mention that I had spent ages in the bin. No wonder squaddies end up in trouble, and employers beware!

I think squaddies from my era and that of my old man are probably the most reliable of people, but I would guess that a few of them have problems.

"Hi John," she shrieked as this big fat guy came into the pub.

He was about my height, must have been twenty stone, big bushy black tash, black hair, and looked a real prick.

She introduced us, and explained that this guy ran a private detective agency across from where our offices were and, in confidence, she explained that she helped with his admin. He was an ex-CID officer from Greater Manchester Police.

Tosser, I thought.

"So ex-army, eh? Why you doing security then?" he asked in a smug voice.

I remember thinking I could just cut his throat, I hated him from the moment I met him. "Why not?" I asked.

"I'm looking for someone to start a security guard department in my business, if you're interested," he blurted out.

I couldn't figure out why he would just come and ask a complete stranger to look at his business. I mean, was the real world so trusting or was I really paranoid? We discussed it at some length and agreed that I would do it. He would pay me cash and provide me with some form of car.

I got the last train to Wigan and the last bus home. I was staying with my parents. It was great. I never go hungry with my mum, that's for sure. I lay in bed that night and tried to understand the dog throttling thing. I must have fallen asleep; it never crossed my mind the next day.

The offices were quite nice, but you could tell his bullshit about value of his company wasn't real. He provided me with a Peugeot 205XS. It was quite sporty. I would spend most of the first few days looking through directories, targeting companies to approach about us providing them with security. He and his fat wife had loads of ideas, but they were all shite.

His 'investigations' were all tracing people that hadn't paid bills to the gas board, or bits of amateur surveillance for brewers who had lost beer kegs and, of course, matrimonial. They were good fun. I went on a couple with him. It was funny that women would come into the office and believe that their husbands or partners were having affairs. Or men would come in hoping that we would prove them to be wrong.

I remember this one case when a relatively wealthy business man called us to his office. He was convinced that she was having an affair. She was twenty years his junior, he was sixty-three.

We left equipped with the statutory photo, and details of his suspicions. Later that day, we followed her from the house to the local gym. She was very pretty, and everything appeared to be in the right place. She drove a merc sports car...yellow! Not hard to follow. When she left the gym, her hair was still wet and she looked rather raunchy.

We followed her to a council housing estate. She pulled in outside a block of flats. Before she got out of the car, a young guy, about thirty, walked out from the doorway of the flats towards the car. He looked thin, even wiry, not handsome, and definitely not well off. He stood outside the car. She got out and started kissing him. John was already taping it all on video. Luckily for us, he obviously lived on the ground-floor flat. We went around the back. The balcony had a gap down each side, big enough to see through and put your arm through if necessary.

Well...how awful. He shagged the arse off her. She obviously loved it rough. He took her from behind and pulled her hair; John taped the lot.

Then, it happened again. I saw myself jump over the balcony, kick the glass door through, and start cutting the guy's throat. I made the woman stay beneath him whilst I cut through. I was pulling his head backwards to make his neck bleed more.

I came out of it in a shiver.

"You okay?" John asked.

"Yes, sorry, it just makes me cringe," I replied.

He looked at me as though I was strange.

The guy in the office was in tears, but he watched the video twice. I found it quite arousing. In fact, I even thought I would go to the gym and offer her my services. I was much fitter and at least more handsome than the other guy.

"I can't believe it, not her, not my wife," he sobbed.

For fuck's sake, I thought, *if he didn't want to know, why the fuck ask us to get it on tape?*

"I thought you would have been glad to know," I said.

John nudged me and shook his head.

"Would you be fucking happy to see your wife getting fucked?" he bawled at me.

"No, but I would be happy that I didn't have to fund her getting fucked anymore!"

"Okay, we'll leave it with you," interrupted John, as he ushered me out of the door.

He tried to lecture me all the way back to the office, but my mind was back in the flat, killing that ugly bastard. I had many hours of confusing dreams, but it obviously wasn't affecting me, because I thought I would know if I was in a state.

When I left the Army, I agreed to go to a regular psychiatric reassessment every six months. I would just have to sit in front of the doctor and reassure him that I was okay, not having bad thoughts about killing myself or anyone else. No problem. Civilian doctors, and in particular psychiatric doctors and nurses, don't really have the time or inclination to take on more clients, unless they are thrust upon them by being sectioned. I was fine, must have never failed an assessment...plus I never had to disclose my issues, as they were governed by the official secrets act...and more!

I had fantastic sex with the guy's wife from the surveillance, exactly as I had imagined it, although, afterwards, I felt guilty. Someone had to die for my pleasure. The poor husband had topped himself and the ugly guy just seemed to do a bunk. Somewhere. I only saw her the once, she was horrible, I hated her, she had made me feel strange. To see her again would have been to try and understand why. No thanks.

Chapter Fifteen

The security department did quite well; we built it up to a few million quid turnover. It was quite easy really. We just had to be honest with people. Tell them what we could and couldn't do. Additional surveillance work at night came included; well, I couldn't really sleep anyway and the dreams when I tried were horrible.

Eventually, John ditched the surveillance, and the tracing bits. I think there was one final job. It was for an oil supply company. They had been ripped off by one of their finance guys. He had embezzled about 4 million quid and then fucked off to Manila in the Philippines. Problem was, once he had got there, he set up a prostitution business and a few other dodgy deals; he had then become homesick. I think he forgot he had a wife and child still in the UK. He had made contact and agreed that if he returned 1 million in cash, they would drop all charges and he could visit his family in the UK without getting arrested.

What a joke. If they wanted to charge or not was irrelevant. They had reported the matter and the government wasn't generally in the practice of forgiveness for such matters. So, we were to go to Manila, collect the cash, provide him with some shitty document, which would convince him that he could come home. It was an anticipated laugh, so three of us went, John, Mark and I. Mark had originally been responsible for the investigation department. He should have been made redundant when it closed, but he was also an ex-copper and they were mates. Thick as thieves, but without the brains.

We landed in Manila, after a great first class flight. We were met by a policeman. He introduced himself as Wan, a friend of Peter (the money man). He drove us to an extremely posh hotel and walked us in. The baggage men took our bags to our individual rooms, all on the top floor, with adjoining doors. We had been booked in for ten days, news to all of us, I think.

"Ten days, John. What the fuck are we going to do for ten days?" asked Mark, the doting husband, who had told his wife it would only take a day or two.

Peter, the money man, he walked up to the reception desk where we were standing. I was amazed. He was a typical accountant-looking guy. Thin, 5'6", balding dark hair, big nose.

"Sorry, gents. I thought you would enjoy the treat of an all-expenses-paid holiday in Manila!"

"Or what, you want to believe it," I said.

John walked over to him and shook his hand. He took care of the formal introductions. It seemed obvious to me that the guy needed the ten days to ensure that he wasn't getting ripped off, that we could indeed supply him with the assurances that he needed before releasing the money. I think Mark was scared of his wife. Don't get me wrong, she was a big girl and you would rather sleep with her than fight her, but a job is a job at the end of the day. They should really have thought themselves lucky that they still had a job.

Anyway, Peter had made all sorts of arrangements for us to have a ball, whilst he obviously carried out his checks. As far as we were aware, that wouldn't be an issue. The first night, although we were all tired from the journey, we decided we would take up Peter's offer of an introduction to Manila's night life. Again, it suited us to the ground. There were no eyes and ears watching what we do here, time to let the hair down.

We were picked up in this American-style limo. The driver was enormous and I always thought Philippinos were all small. He was very polite, called us sir all the time, insisted on opening and closing the doors, etc. He drove for about forty minutes around the town, the nice areas and the not so nice. It seemed that every road, every corner had their own prostitutes and they certainly weren't backwards in coming forward. The driver would stop quite often just to show us the response at our vehicle. It was amazing. These poor people would do almost anything for money. We ended up at a glitzy looking night club. After the door man had finished his chat with our driver, we were escorted past the crowds of locals, through the dancing public, into the rear section of the club. It was great; there was quite a large table, with comfy leather chairs around it. Yes, it was for us.

We sat down, glancing and laughing at each other. I was surprised; the music was very much the same as you would get at home in a night club, except you couldn't understand a word the DJ was on about. Another, smaller man came over to the table with a big smile on his face.

"You would like some champagne?" he asked.

"How much is it?" replied John.

"All your drinks and entertainment have already been taken care of, sir," he replied.

Wow, now that's service, obviously a million pounds in the Philippines is worth a lot more than in the UK.

"Yes, we will all have champagne," John responded.

The man went away and returned with three bottles of vintage Krug. Not the best, but hey; it was free and I suppose it's not easy to get hold of it over on this side of the world.

We all sat talking in whispers about the odd pretty Philippine girl that went past and were just cracking open the third bottle when another enormous fat geezer walked over to our table. He walked behind John and put his hands on John's shoulders. He started massaging him.

"What are you doing?" demanded John.

"Part of service sir, help you make relaxed," he replied.

It was amazing, John eventually settled down, but didn't look overly pleased when the woman walked over and did my shoulders.

"Maybe they think you're gay," I said.

"Well, actually you think that's a woman massaging your shoulders, think again buddy," he laughed.

He was right; it was a hermaphrodite, or Kye –Tie. Basically a person with both sexual organs.

"Could be interesting," I joked.

"Please tell me you're joking," said Mark, joining in the conversation.

"Of course I am, you walley."

About one thirty in the morning, we all agreed it was time to go and murder that jet lag. Our driver re-appeared and we again were escorted through the crowds to the car. We expressed our gratitude to the manager and got back into the car. I think we had driven about two miles and Mark shouted, "Stop the car!"

I was scared stiff. Apart from him wanting to be sick, I couldn't imagine any reason for the panic.

"Reverse," he shouted, obviously drunk.

And there she was, the woman of his dreams, standing on a street corner looking like a lost lamb.

"Do you think she would be available to spend the night with me?" asked Mark, speaking to the driver.

The driver got out of the car and walked up to the girl. He spoke for a few seconds and came back. "How long you want her for?" he asked.

"Forever," replied Mark.

I was in bits, I couldn't stop laughing.

"Fuck off, Mark. She isn't that nice," said John.

"I don't care, I think she's fabulous," explained Mark.

The driver went back to the girl and said something to her. She laughed and walked over to the car.

"Who want me forever?" she asked.

"That will be me then," replied Mark.

She got into the car, next to Mark. He was like a big kid. I must say she was very pretty, but something wasn't quite right. Anyway, we were all pissed, I'm sure he would sort it out in the morning.

I slept reasonably well through the first night, probably helped by the journey and the masses of champagne we had consumed. I went across to the breakfast bar, on the roof of the hotel. John was there reading a British newspaper.

"Morning," I greeted him.

"All right mate, did you sleep? he asked.

"Like a baby. What about you?" I asked.

"Well, it would have been better if he hadn't been going on with her for half the night and then yapping on for hours."

Mark arrived about twenty minutes after we had finished our breakfast. He looked absolutely knackered, but with a beaming smile on his face. He had obviously enjoyed the company and very quickly had forgotten his quest to get home early. Well, I suppose from our point of view that would make his little affair worthwhile.

"You're a noisy twat," snarled John.

"Hey! Keep the jealousy to yourself. I think I'm in love," he replied.

"How much did you pay her?" I asked.

"Nothing yet. I've asked her to stay with me until we leave," he replied.

"You're not all there. Have you at least asked what she is going to charge you?" asked John.

"No, the driver told me not to worry about it, Peter was paying," he replied.

I couldn't believe my eyes when two minutes later his mistress walked out onto the terrace to join us. She had a silky dressing gown on, her hair was perfectly kemp, and she did look rather fresh faced.

"How old is she?" I asked hurriedly as she was approaching.

"Must be about twenty-two," replied Mark.

She sat down next to Mark and kissed him on the cheek. She looked at John and I and smiled with a perfectly innocent smile. "Hello, I am Silim," she announced in her broken English.

"Hi, I'm John, and this is Reachard," announced John.

She smiled and sat looking at Mark.

"You eat?" he asked.

"Yes, please sir," she replied.

"I'm going before I throw up," I told them.

John joined me and we started to walk off. We agreed with Mark to meet about lunchtime, as we had agreed to meet Peter at two.

I was sitting enjoying the heat when the others arrived, Mark with what appeared to be a permanent smile on his face.

"Peter won't be coming," John announced. "He said for us to just do whatever we wanted until we heard from him; he would sort out any bills, as long as we didn't buy anything stupid, like boats or cars. Oh and he arranged for the driver to take us to a variety of different restaurants and night clubs over the next few nights."

He was becoming more bizarre by the moment, but never waste an opportunity. For the next six days we had a ball. Mark had his dream lady hanging off him everywhere he went; John and I just enjoyed the experience. We both concluded that we certainly weren't going to be roped into any girls, as we needed to keep our wits about us.

The morning before we left, Peter finally showed his face at the breakfast table.

"Okay boys, everything is in place for your flight tomorrow. I'll bring you a case each, which you need to keep with you at all times, and when you arrive in Heathrow, a member of the company will come and sign for each one individually. Is there anything I can do to help you guys enjoy your last night here?"

"No, thanks. We have had a ball, thanks," replied John.

"Actually, Peter, I have a question," said Mark.

"What's that, Mark?" replied Peter.

"I think I've fallen in love with this girl and I want to take her home with me."

John and I looked at each other and burst out laughing.

"You're fucking married," laughed John.

"I don't care; I want to take her away from all this. I'll let her stay in a flat until I work out what I'm going to do."

"How old is she?" asked Peter.

"No idea. I think she's about twenty-two," replied Mark

Peter spoke to her in her native tongue for a couple of minutes. He then turned and looked at Mark. "Bad news I'm afraid, Mark. She doesn't have a passport," he declared.

"Well, can't we get her one?" he asked.

"Not until she reaches the age of sixteen," he said.

Well, Mark turned white; he looked at us all individually seeking help. "How old is she?" he asked.

"Thirteen," declared Peter.

It was suggested that he sort her out financially and have the driver return her home…never to be spoken about again.

Chapter Sixteen

We arrived back in Heathrow and were met by the said company representatives, who, as per protocol, gave us receipts, counted the money, and left us. We travelled on to Manchester, and upon arriving at customs, one of the officers asked Mark for a word. He was cacking himself, but it was purely to ask if he had realized that his passport was due to expire within the month. Funny enough, he never volunteered for any trips in the future, and I imagine he's probably still very happily married to his fat wife.

I kept having those strange dreams though. I found myself struggling with all kinds of situations. Whilst work was okay, John was a bit of a tit. I think he had these great visions of grandeur, but certainly didn't have the brains to do it alone. He eventually got rid of Mark and started keeping his thick wife out of things. She really was Mrs. Bucket!

Out of the blue, I received a call on the business phone. It was Harvey's wife. Never thought I would hear from her again. She was lovely, telling me that she had settled down again, that she was expecting another child, that her husband was Catholic. I don't know why, but that made me feel a little uneasy. Although things had settled somewhat over there, well, Adams and McGuiness were finally getting away with their lies, I still had a horrible feeling about it all. She told me that everybody that had known me before the incident thought I had died. It was only a week previously that she had bumped into John Clune, another former colleague from the unit and he explained that whilst I had lived, the Army had decided that I should leave under a new identity. It was the best chance I had of having any form of normal life, which in Army terms meant; Oh shit! We have lost control of this one, get rid of him.

She was telling me about the punishment beatings that went on nowadays by the IRA and people that suffered crime would call their local IRA man rather than the RUC, who would deal with things more severely. Cheeky shits, they really think that you can run local communities on fear. It's pathetic, even if we were stupid enough to allow a re-united Ireland (which Tony Blair probably would if he wasn't sure he would be on a world-wide death list, like nothing he knows, nothing like these amateur Arab terrorists!), the Guardia wouldn't allow such crap to go on either. Adams and McGuiness are and always have been a pair of murdering, lying bastards. I can't believe the Catholic community are blind enough to believe anything they say. I mean I have met a large number of Irish Catholics and I must say they are peace-loving, genuine people, most with better personal values than I could ever wish to have, so I just don't get it.

Anyway, it was great to hear from her and we ended the conversation with me promising to visit her over there.

John suddenly, overnight decided he wanted to sell the company. *Well, great,* I thought. *I go and get all the business, manage it all to this stage and he and his wife sell it, leave us to our destiny, whilst he and his dragon get all the rewards. Well, fuck you,* I thought.

I started doing my own little thing. I started carrying out private surveillances again, doing a little retribution work for disgruntled housewives and husbands. It was fun and good money. The dreams though!

I was setting off to Liverpool to give a prostitute's handler a bit of a slap, as he had been beating her. Her husband knew she was a hooker, but didn't like her handler. The night before, I had had some really frightening dreams.

I pulled into the overflow car park behind the Royal Liverpool Hospital; this was her patch. I must say, if I had to pay for sex, she would have been right up there with the choices. She was really gorgeous. I suppose hence her having so much trouble. I saw her walking down the road. She had on a very short leather skirt; a white top, which was also very revealing; high heels; loads of make-up; and a black hand bag thrown over her shoulder. She was so obviously on the game.

A black Audi pulled up next to her. I couldn't see the driver, but I assumed it was a punter. She leaned over into the driver's window. After a brief conversation, she walked around and got into the passenger seat. The car pulled off and headed towards me. It turned into the car park and pulled in about twenty yards behind me. How convenient.

As soon as the engine was switched off, her head disappeared out of sight and the passenger seemed to be trying to lean backwards. No prizes for guessing.

It didn't last for long. She re-appeared. He got out of the car. He must have been fifty to sixty, very well dressed in a dark blue suit, his shirt open at the top, with a bright red tie open around his neck. He adjusted himself, looked around and got back into the car. I could see both their heads. I assume he was just passing the time he had paid for.

Another car pulled in, almost next to them. It was a black-and-white 4 x 4, one of those smaller ones, but it had obviously had a lot of money spent on it. It had massive wheels and tires. It also had a bull or something painted on the spare wheel on the back.

I watched as a black guy got out. He didn't look overly big, but was tall, about 6'2". He was wearing a pair of jeans, a white, open neck shirt and a black jacket over the top. He walked over to the car and leaned into the driver's window. It a was quiet for a couple of minutes, then the girl got out and started screaming at him over the car. The driver of the Audi obviously wanted no part of this and drove off in rather a hurry.

The black guy was shouting at her and pointing. He launched himself toward her and grabbed her by the hair. I felt really strange. I got out of the car. He looked over at me.

"What the fuck are you looking at?" he shouted.

I couldn't speak. I felt my face really flush, and I had a headache. I had that weird vision of strangling the puppy in my mind and it was making me dead angry. I couldn't control it any more.

He was unconscious on the floor and I was still hitting him. She was screaming. I stopped. She was more scared of me than she had been of him. I couldn't figure out what had happened. I went back to the car. Before I got in, she had stopped screaming.

"Ssshh." I put my finger to my mouth and indicated. I then got back into the car and drove off. I was laughing on the way home, I don't know why, or at what. But I had the music up loud, and I was laughing.

It was in the papers in the morning.

"A man was found severely beaten in the grounds of the Royal Liverpool Hospital last night. Police believe it was a drugs-related incident and are requesting information from any members of the public who either witnessed or have heard anything. The man is in a critical condition. If you wish to help, call Merseyside Police on 0151 777 6140 or anonymous crime stoppers on 0800…"

Hmmm, not quite to plan, but hey, who cares. I phoned the husband

"That what you wanted?" I asked.

"You're a fucking lunatic!" he replied.

"My misses is more scared of you than her pimp. I'll sort the money out today, but what happens if he dies?" he asked.

"As long as you keep your mouth shut, there is only us that knows about it, so who cares, he is a shit bag anyway," I explained.

"Oh, okay, then," he answered apprehensively.

"You haven't told your wife about it, I assume," I asked.

"No, no, I won't," he answered.

I wasn't sure about him; I would have to be careful. Maybe I would have to lean on him a little to make sure, I thought to myself.

I received the money and a little more. He said the extra was to make sure that I didn't go looking for him. Strange guy.

The sale of the business was going well one minute and then crap the next. He was selling to the biggest and wealthiest in the world. The managing director of the company seemed okay and ex-Royal Artillery Colonel. I don't think he had enough power to conclude the deal, without going back to his American bosses though. I think once they had done their due diligence, the order was to mess us about and get the price down to the lowest possible. The problem with a strategy like that was simple. The clients were also being messed about, which reflected poorly on the organization buying. But they just couldn't see it.

I found it quite stressful. I haven't mentioned it, but I got married in the meantime to lovely young girl, really homely. I thought that was what I needed to settle down, etc.

Three weeks after the prostitute affair, I got a call from the husband or boyfriend, whatever he was. He was beside himself.

"What's up?" I asked.

"They have fucking killed her, that's what's up. She's dead!" he replied.

She had been found murdered on a layby next to the East Lancs. Road. The road runs between Liverpool, Skelmersdale in Lancashire, Rainford and St. Helens. Really good choice of place. All the local shaggers went there and loads of different vehicles would be parked at different times during the night. The layby is sort of U-shaped, with the entrance at one end and the exit at the other, surrounded by trees and shrubs.

I calmed him down and assured him that once things had settled, I would meet him personally and we would sort this out.

In reality, I didn't want to get involved.

The black guy had recovered in the hospital, but was still in there. So he must have arranged it from his hospital bed. If I were to go and speak to him, he would obviously recognize me and I would be right in it.

My dad had been diagnosed with kidney failure. That was really bad news. It meant he had to go to the Royal three times a week for dialysis. Poor guy. He was such a rock. I mean, my poor mum, she had been the loyal housewife and mother to us all as far back as I can remember and now he would take some looking after. Never mind, she would cope...she always did! I had to be careful when dealing with Liverpool; my eldest brother was in the police, and whilst the police aren't the brightest buttons in the box, he had a tendency to know what I was up to, or more like when I was up to something, he seemed to know.

Not too long after that incident, I was having a drink in that railway pub in Warrington one night; there weren't many faces around the bar, so everybody stood out for their own insignificant reasons. I still had a habit of making sure I could recognize all the faces present, every time I went into a pub.

On this particular evening, I noticed two faces that I recognized instantly, but I couldn't quite place where I knew them from. It would annoy me for hours, and the mere fact that it troubled me so much forced me into the unusual mistake of looking far too long at a group of people. Eventually and inevitably one of the two stared back at me, as if to acknowledge that he had noted me looking.

He seemed to click that he knew me and looked worried. He whispered something to his mate, who slowly, but obviously turned around to look. He turned away immediately, put his pint down, nudged the other guy by the arm, and walked directly towards the door.

I was intrigued, not really worried, but I wouldn't have slept well if I hadn't have gone to try and find out who they were. I also rushed to the door. I caught the last one by his arm. He was wearing a canvas jacket. The jacket was loose, and as I pulled on his arm, I noticed a holster hanging quite loose underneath. It certainly wasn't British traditional issue gear either.

"Hey, I know you, don't I?"

"No, you don't. Now fuck off and leave me alone," he snarled with his broad Belfast accent.

I froze. Oh shit, now I remembered who they were, they were both members of PIRA. What were they doing in Warrington? What on earth would attract them to here? They were obviously still part of the IRA's Liverpool ASU, so what were they doing in Warrington? Maybe it was a relatively relaxed town, relaxed enough for them to expose themselves and go out for a pint together. No, not even Warrington was that safe for them.

Well, I didn't have to guess for long.

A policeman tried to stop them just after they left the pub. They drove from the pub car park (next door to the police station), to the main traffic lights, turned right. About three hundred yards later a policeman tried to stop them. I believe they opened fire. Well, someone certainly did. I got into my car and drove home.

Unfortunately, the rest of their guys were a little more professional; callous, but professional. The remainder of the story is now part of Warrington's history, and best left alone. It's never good to talk about incidents that involve children.

CHAPTER SEVENTEEN

I went over to Belfast. I flew into the Harbour airport; I thought it would make me feel a little easier. We had always used Aldergrove. I walked through the airport and immediately noticed Denise standing there. She rushed toward me and gave me a big hug.

"My, you've put weight on," she kindly remarked.

"Thanks, and you have shrunk," I replied.

She drove us into Belfast, where we went into a bar-come-hotel thing. Everything seemed so different, so relaxed. It was bizarre. I booked in and put my gear into my room. She waited at the bar. She was funny, she would try and drink at the same rate that men drink, knowing full well she couldn't handle it.

"I've asked my friends to come along later. They are all dying to meet you," she said in a questioning sort of way.

"Fine," I replied.

We chatted for about two hours, whilst pouring ourselves champagne and brandy. I used to love this drink, but could never remember at what point one should stop. We were both pissed by the time her friends arrived and the bar was pretty full. I felt really proud of myself. I hadn't even noticed the bar filling up. I must have been getting used to the fact that I was a civilian. We drank all night. There was a kind of disco in the background, which kept the spirits up, all old fashioned music.

At elevenish, the guy behind the bar said, "We are about to close, but you can use the resident's bar upstairs if you like."

Great and off we went. By this time, our party was about fifteen people, either friends of theirs that happened to have been passing, or blokes trying to cop off with her mates. Either way, it was all pleasant. Upstairs was quite big and there were already a few people there. In particular, there were five guys at the end of the bar, which automatically looked suspicious to me. They started staring and whispering to one another.

After an hour, I went to the toilet. I was immediately conscious that one of them followed. I went to the urinal nearest to the door, and pushed my pee out as quickly as possible. I was just shaking as he walked through the door. I spun around. He nearly fell over.

"What's wrong with you?" I asked.

"Now't, you scared me," he answered.

"You have been staring at me all night, what's the score?"

"Nothing, honest. Billy thought he recognized you, that's all."

Well, the name Billy usually meant that it wasn't much to worry about, they were obviously prods. I shook the guy's hand as though we were old mates, and went back to the bar. I watched as he returned from the toilet and went back to his friends.

They seemed to huddle together and then all looked over. I raised my glass as though to toast them, then turned away. I knew they would come over.

As predicted, they all came over. Billy, the biggest of them, spoke to me.

"I'm sure I know you," he said.

"I'm sure you do," I answered.

"Aren't you Topper?" he asked.

Well, I was terrified. I just stared at him.

"Don't worry, you're safe with us. We know the score. You're a friend of Eric McKinley's," he said.

"How do you know Eric?" I asked apprehensively.

"From his dad's club," he said.

Eric's dad was the proprietor of a loyalist club in Castlereigh. I had been there before. We used to call it the metal door club, named so because the external door was reinforced steel. It also had another door inside that was equally as difficult to get through. Great place. With the picture of the queen on the wall and no women allowed, it was a real old fashioned drinking man's pub.

"Shall I give him a ring?" he asked.

"Yes, go on," I replied. I would have been astounded if he could get hold of him.

He spoke to someone for a few minutes. "He's coming over," he said.

Well, would you believe it? I hadn't seen Eric for years. He was a really good friend. He was involved in some amazing things whilst working with us, but the less said the better on this occasion. He hadn't changed a bit. He always used to look a bit of a poser. Denise knew him, which made things a little easier.

"How did you meet these thugs?" he asked with a beaming smile.

"They were staring at me when I walked in, and kept whispering," I replied.

"Think yourselves lucky to be alive," he told them. "Topper used to kill you if you stared at him long enough," he explained.

We drank and drank. About 3 o'clock, Denise said she felt awful and had to go for a lie down. She asked if she could use my room. I escorted her inside, where she instantly collapsed onto the bed, I mean out! I undressed her completely, knickers and all, and put her into the bed. See, she was a friend; the sex stuff never even crossed my mind. Just for a moment it reminded me of the time in the hotel where I got snatched. I wondered if that's how those IRA guys felt when they thought I was about to bed their mate's girlfriend.

I returned to the party, as that was what it obviously was now. Denise's friend, Lynn was also looking a little worse for wear. She too ended up in my bed, naked. I remember thinking, *my God, their bits are the same color and shape.* I wondered did that mean they were the same inside. After deciding I was pissed, I again returned to the party. A black guy stood next to Eric.

He was introduced as Spook. Apparently, he had been one of the IRA's primary drug dealers in the past. Strange, I had never heard of him, plus, I had never seen a black man associated with the IRA before.

All of a sudden, I had one of those flash dreams; it was cats this time though. I was watching a cat in a glass-fronted oven. It was getting hotter and hotter. The cat could see me and was obviously expressing its discomfort. It was making my teeth clench with anger, but I think it was me that had put the cat in the oven, and I wanted it to die!

"Topper!" Eric shouted.

"Sorry, I was miles away," I told him.

"Seen that look before," said Spook. "I know what you need. Come with me," he said.

We walked off to the toilets. He was medium build, bald, but quite fresh-faced looking. I reckon he must have been in his late thirties, quite well spoken though. Once in the toilet, he pulled out a small, black wallet, and removed a small amount of what was obviously cocaine.

"You're joking," I said.

"No, actually, I used to supply all your guys, the RUC guys that is. Don't worry, it doesn't make you a junkie. A few of your guys have similar problems, and when they take this, it tends to relax them. Just try it," he said.

Well, I suppose I hadn't anything to lose. I had never taken cocaine before, so it was something new. I certainly knew it wouldn't be a regular thing; my brother would murder me if he knew.

He chopped it up with a credit card and put into about four lines. He rolled up a twenty pound note, and sniffed a whole row at once. I gathered that was his way of showing me that it was good enough for him, and it wasn't dangerous. He rolled a separate twenty and passed it too me. "Just sniff it in all at once," he said.

I did a row. It just felt like sniffing dust. He nodded at me to do another, whilst he started preparing more. After we had done quite a bit, we returned to the bar. I didn't feel any different, or I didn't think I did.

There was a guy standing in the place where I had stood. He looked completely non-descript. He must have been 5'9", dark curly hair, and fair complexion, looked quite civil in his brown trousers, brown shirt, and khaki jacket.

"Who are you?" I asked.

"Just a local come in for a drink," he replied.

"Fucking liar, you from the police?" I said aggressively, not really knowing why I had said it.

"Calm down, Topper," said Spook.

"He's here to keep an eye on us. Tell him to fuck off or I'll kill him," I said. At that point, somewhere in my mind I thought, *Maybe this cocaine has affected me.*

The guy was quite passive and moved further down the bar. It didn't stop my paranoia though; I couldn't stop staring at him.

About an hour later, I hadn't noticed that he had again joined our group. I looked across and watched him. He was laughing at people's jokes and comments, but not participating. I remembered that role. He was obviously at work. I watched him some more. He had a bottle of beer in his hand. He kept putting it to his mouth, but it never got any emptier. He was obviously working for someone.

The cocaine took over. "See, I told you, that prick is working for someone, gathering information on you, Spook," I shouted.

The guy stepped back. I launched myself at him, knocking him to the ground. I immediately gripped with his throat with my right hand. He couldn't move. I was trying to kill him.

It must have taken about five of the others to eventually get me off him; just as he was starting to lose consciousness. Spook and Eric got the guy up off the floor.

"You fucking ask him where he's from," I bellowed.

"Okay, Topper, calm down. I'll find out," said Eric.

They asked him a few questions. He kept indicating that Spook knew him, or that he should, as he was local to him. He said they had often passed each other in the street.

"He's lying. Let's take him for a ride," I said in my weird state.

"Okay, Topper, calm down. It's not like that anymore," replied Eric.

Spook advised the guy to leave and not to return. He also told him that if he found that he had been lying, he would track him down and sort him out. The guy was ever so grateful, and then left.

I vaguely remember Spook using his mobile phone

We were still at the bar at six in the morning. I realized I was fully awake. In fact, I was buzzing! "So, this is the effect that cocaine has on you, eh!" I said to Spook.

"You like it?" he asked.

"Oh, do I," I sang.

"Good. I've put a little something in your pocket for your journey," he said.

"What journey?" I asked.

"I think you had best go home today...for all our sakes," he answered.

"I think it's best, Topper," said Eric.

I suppose they were right. I didn't belong here. The guy at the bar probably was a police officer and they probably knew it. The last thing they needed was some ex-psycho getting the heat turned on them. I'm sure they knew what they were doing. I went back to my room.

Lynn was already up. She was just finishing getting dressed. "Topper, I'll have to go. I've got to pick up my kids," she explained.

"That's okay. It's lovely to have met you," I answered.

She hugged me and left.

I was knackered. I got undressed to my undies and got into bed next to Denise.

When I woke it was just after one. I felt like shit. Denise was sat fully dressed in a chair, reading the papers.

"You okay?" she asked.

"No, I'm fucking not," I mumbled.

"You're gonna feel a lot worse when you see the news," she said. She switched the telly on. 'About eight this morning, the body of a young man was found hanging on a building site just outside the city center. The man had been beaten and strangled. Sources believe he had been interrogated by one of the local terrorist organizations. The police are refusing to release any further details.

"What's that about?" I asked her.

"You tell me," she said.

"I don't understand," I told her.

"I got a call from Eric about 9 o'clock; he said that this guy had been fingered by you. That you had told Spook that he was a policeman trying to get at him. Spook had made a call when you weren't looking, and then advised the guy to leave. "What happened after I went to bed?" she asked.

I gave her a vague run down of what had gone on after she had left. She was horrified. "We need to get you to the airport as soon as possible," she said.

"I haven't done anything," I said.

"That doesn't matter. Eric said the guy was a member of the UDA. He was trying to find out who Spook was supplying within the IRA. The UDA won't be very happy that you fingered him." She sounded frantic.

"But I'm on their side," I said.

"Won't look like that to them. I know Eric is trying to sort it through his dad, but in the meantime, let's get you out of here."

Great, I thought. I was at the airport within the hour. I sat waiting for my flight, trying to remember everything that had gone on. Denise was strutting up and down the airport like she was really worried.

"Denise, you get out of here. I'll be okay now," I told her.

"Okay, but ring me when you arrive in Liverpool," she demanded.

We hugged and I promised to call her. Whilst sitting thinking about things, I remembered Spook had said something about something in my pocket. I felt something screwed up and took it out. It was twenty quid. I unscrewed it and saw the rather large piece of cocaine. I felt the blood drain from my face. I took it to the toilet and flushed it away. Fuck sake! God knows what would have happened if I had been caught with that at Liverpool airport. I arrived home safely amd rang Denise.

"I think Eric's sorted it," she said.

I went to bed and slept for around eighteen hours. I must have been exhausted. I wondered who that guy had been. Surely not internal services. He was far too indiscreet. He must have been a player for the UDA, as Eric had said. Well, you live and you learn…or not.

I started to feel really ill some weeks later. My dad was doing his dialysis on an every-other-day basis and we could see it was winding him up.

He had a driver though, which made life a little easier for him. The guy would drive him to the Royal and bring him back after the dialysis. It was strange to see my dad looking so ill. I mean, we had seen him go through some injuries during our childhood, but never really ill. I remember when we were quite young, he got blown up on military exercise. He was with the Artillery then. 27 Medium Regiment, based in Germany. Great days, they were. Everybody took care of everybody else, a real sense of community spirit. Some of the guys my dad worked with in the Artillery. I later came to work with them when I joined the same Regiment. But, instead of calling them uncle this and Uncle that, I was calling them Sir or Sarge, etc. What a strange turn of events, but even all these years later, we stay in touch, and it's still like a family.

Chapter Eighteen

Touché!

I think I must have been about ten.

In the Army, as a dependant, the worst possible case scenario is a black staff car pulling up outside your house and the padre getting out. He's always the bearer of bad news. That American film, the one where the brothers are all involved in the Second World War. 'Saving Private Ryan',

The scene when the staff car pulls up outside the mother's house–I felt that was really touching.

I wasn't there when the staff car arrived outside our house, but I do remember after it had left my mum trying desperately to hide her emotions. I recall her and my eldest brother going off to see my dad in hospital. The rest of us weren't told too much. A few weeks later, my mum sat us down and explained that he had been blown up.

I later established for myself what had happened. Part of his role was to get rid of the excess charge bags, unused after firing. A charge bag is a large cloth bag of explosive powder that is put into the barrel of an artillery gun. It follows the shell which gets projected thirty kilometres or so by the charge bag. It's the exploding charge bag that propels the shell. You can imagine how dangerous they are. In the bad old days, when they had finished live firing in the Artillery, someone would pile up the charge bags, put a line of powder to the pile, and once a safe distance away, light the powder. Inevitably, the pile would burn at some ridiculous heat, and thus be deemed extremely dangerous.

Apparently, in my father's case, whomever had laid the trail of powder had used the wrong powder. They had used black powder, which burns a lot quicker than the stuff meant to be used. So the principle of lighting the powder train, and then walking (not running) to a safe distance had gone by the wayside. Within seconds of him lighting the powder trail, the charge bags ignited, allowing no time for him to get to a safe distance, thus setting him on fire. From what I heard from his colleagues, he was completely ablaze. They had to roll him in the sand to try and get the flames out. His skin was burning as well as his clothes.

We only got to see him a few months after it had happened. We went to a military hospital in the town of Iserlohn in West Germany. Prior to being permitted to see him, we were told to put on sterile gowns and masks. We entered this room, which, believe me, didn't smell very nice. There in the corner, on a bed, was this black man. His hands appeared to be tied up in the air with plastic bags around them.

As we got closer, you could see a little slit, which was a cut in the facial skin put in by the doctors so he could see. There was another slit, which I think was his mouth. It was awful. But still, he was alive. We were told that he would recover, but he would have a different face. I couldn't wait. How weird would that be? When he did eventually recover, his face hadn't changed at all. In fact, the only difference was that a scar he had received during a parachuting accident some years prior had been burnt away. All that and still the same face.

Oh well, he was still our dad, that was the main thing.

Years later, he used to tell us about the dialysis. It sounded fascinating. Not something I believe everybody could cope with. Well, certainly not me.

I was struggling with my dreams; I was getting into fights in pubs with horrible effect; and I was sure that I wasn't going to get away with it for much longer. One day I found myself taking painkillers for a splitting headache. I just kept taking them. I must have taken around thirty when my mum came in. I collapsed. I remember being in hospital, where everybody kept looking at me as though I were a loon. I suppose for all intents and purposes I was.

The doctor came over and told me I would be all right, but he would like me to voluntarily admit myself to the psychiatric wing for evaluation. I agreed, knowing if I didn't, they would probably section me.

It was great being away from the real world. No worries, only visitors when you wanted them. Sex whenever or if ever you wanted. Best of all were the tablets. I would take one, then for the next hour feel like I was walking on cotton wool; it was great. The big difference was, I was able to predict before I had one of my wobblies, and I knew my mind would take me a place I didn't want to go to. That may sound bizarre, but that's how it happened. So I could tuck myself away and get on with it.

I stayed there for a while.

On the last meeting I had in hospital, the main man told me I had a severe personality disorder. I mean, I had never spoken to this guy, he had never evaluated me, but he thought he knew what my problem was!

I thought he was just being rude, so I chose to ignore it. He never said I needed treatment, and I certainly hadn't told them about the past. I went on my way.

I had been out of hospital for just under a week when one of our previous clients from the security company called me and asked me to meet him in a pub in Warrington. Lovely guy, called Ron. He had previously been the finance director of a cooker company we used to deal with. He had since left and was working for a large public transport company in Liverpool. He said he wanted me to come and look at the security of this public transport company. He knew I had been having problems recently, and wanted me to know that he would get me to do the job on a consultancy basis, but it was because he thought I could do the job, not because he felt sorry for me. I felt humbled like never before.

I went to the offices on Edge Lane in Liverpool. He introduced me to the chairman, Peter; the commercial director, Dominic; and a few others. It seemed like an okay setup. But immediately you could see his concerns. The chairman seemed a little weak and the commercial director a little 'rum'.

I asked him if I could spend the first few weeks just looking around and getting to meet people. Thus I would get a feel for what was going on.

The guy currently responsible for security was a guy called Steve. He was the health and safety manager. Coincidentally, the contract security was provided by the large company that had bought John's security company. He was now running it for them. What a small and unfortunate world. It was great. A copper's dream. You didn't have to look far to find things wrong, there was so much–from expense claims, to equipment thefts, from fuel thefts, to the illegal buying and selling of buses. It was amazing. I could see from the outset that I wasn't welcomed by the majority of staff. Although I have to give credit for a change to the Transport and General Workers Union and unison; they were really quite helpful.

I remember I had to meet the bus inspectors or their boss and evaluate their effectiveness throughout the company. Well, their poor manager, Charlie, had been given a job without any form of policy or procedures, no targets or direction. They weren't a waste of time, but were very quickly becoming the target for redundancies. The question for us was did we retrain them, or get rid of them. The choice was mine.

I was offered a tidy sum to recruit my own team, and to stay on as security manager. I thought long and hard about it, but concluded that these guys deserved a chance, which to my surprise, once given, they seemed to grasp with both hands.

We had fun. We reduced assaults from an average of 40 per month to 2, theft incidents from 180 to 21, criminal damage to buses from over 300 incidents to 25. It went well.

Unfortunately, we also had to deal with the local transport authority, Mersey travel–so old fashioned and set in their ways, publicly funded and no real direction. They hated anything positive that they weren't responsible for dealing with. Then those poor fuckers–having to deal with me; Bolshy, overconfident and, fuck, I could be aggressive if I wanted to be.

In contrast, the police were great. They were supportive, enjoyed new initiatives, got on board with anything that would have a positive impact on crime. We had some great achievements together.

One in particular got some good coverage in the local press, *The Echo*. Bus drivers going into Kirkby were being robbed by lads with knives. Having a basic understanding of the lack of police resources, we decided that we would contribute by mounting our own operation. Sounds like fun? Oh, it was. We organized a bogus bus, fitted with hidden CCTV cameras throughout. We had one of our guys, Steve drive it. One guy, Arthur, would be on the bus, pretending to be drunk, then three cars with two or three in each car would shadow the bus. The original bus would stop service before Kirkby, and ours would run the remainder of the route.

Two-thirds of the way through the route, two lads got on the bus. They looked apprehensive and suspicious. As the bus pulled away, one of them went to see Arthur. He looked him over and obviously concluded that he was a drunk.

The other was later seen on the video pulling an enormous knife out of his jacket and threaten Steve the driver. To cut a long and naughty story short, they both got arrested. One was sentenced to five years, the other to five and a half. It was a good result. The lads got commendations from the Chief Constable and from the courts.

Arthur took us to a night club called Reds, which was just up the road from the bus company offices along Edge Lane. As we entered, I noticed the head doorman had a face that I recognized. It was Jimmy Price. He boxed in the boycotted Olympics in Kenya in the eighties. I remember because he beat the Kenyan in the finals. He had won Commonwealth Gold at the games. He also went on to box professionally for Frank Warren, but allegedly fell foul of the Warren scams.

We got on like a house on fire; he was fun and seemed to understand my sick sense of humour. We would later become very good mates. He introduced me to some great people, like Panama, a south Liverpool chap who ran security companies. He had done a life sentence for murdering his wife. John Haas also ran security companies, and later became famous for scamming the Home Secretary on the Arms for sentence deal, along with Tony Bennett. Jimmy was a great help dealing with the crime on the buses, as he was quite well known in South Liverpool.

We had a few arrangements that would ensure that very little trouble was experienced on our buses whilst passing through his areas. In the Speke area of Liverpool, we had another good friend of Jimmy's helping us with sorting matters out, Tony Sinnett...God bless his soul. He was later murdered. Tony ensured that there was no naughtiness with our competitors. Anyway, very quickly, we secured most of the public transport in Liverpool. Mersey Travel hated me for it. They don't really give a toss about public safety, just about themselves. To think the amount of staff and general resources they have, compared to the amount of money they receive, well it's ridiculous. A private company could have achieved twice as much at a third of the cost.

Pathetic.

We later had some rather corrupt dealings with the new director general of Mersey Travel, Neil Scales, who later tried to bankrupt me. Oh, and your clock is still ticking, Mr. Scales! The job was good fun. We carried out surveillances by night and controlled bus incidents by day. It was like a private police force.

I think it must have been after month five I started getting my funny dreams again. Strange how they had gone and then suddenly came back. They were more distinct now, more specific. I kept feeling the urge to go along with them, as though they were becoming an essential guide in my life. For the first time since leaving the army, I decided to tell someone about them. Jimmy, he was great. He seemed to understand and they didn't faze him at all. In fact, whenever I did have the urge to carry out one of the dreams, he would help me to do so. We beat the shit out of anyone who wouldn't play the game; it was a great stress relief. The best thing was we didn't need to kill anyone. Maybe this was me getting older, but the urge wasn't there. We used to take it in turns. He would go with the boys one night and sort a problem, then ring me at two A.M., to say "the eagle has landed"–that meant the matter was sorted.

Likewise I would go on my own and sort other problems and likewise would make the same call to him. Good interesting days those.

Chapter Nineteen

Out of the blue, a few months into my employ with the public transport company, I received a call from an old army colleague.

"Hi Topper, Spike here!"

Well, I couldn't believe it. After so many years, so much change, I thought he was dead.

"Hi Spike, where are you?" I asked.

"In Belfast, I'm working privately," he replied.

"For who?" I asked.

"I'll tell you that when you come over," he replied.

I was naturally intrigued; I would obviously have to go, even if just to see how, or if, he had changed. I booked a flight from Liverpool to Belfast International, as it is now known. I made arrangements for him to meet me at the airport. He said I didn't need to book a hotel, so I didn't.

I landed in Belfast. It was a strange feeling. After so much time spent here, so much concern about whom was watching, listening or following, it would be hard to switch off.

The airport was modern. It didn't look much like it had previously; in fact the place looked 100 percent better. I noticed the police wandering around, like they do in most other British airports. They all looked so young. A rather large policeman was staring at me. I tried to avoid his stare. I don't know why, perhaps it was instinct.

"Are you okay, sir?" he asked in a brash Northern Irish accent.

"Yes, fine. Why?" I replied.

"No problem, sir. You just look a bit confused. Are you sure you're okay?"

I ignored him and walked away. I was immediately conscious that he was following me and using his radio. I became nervous, although I hadn't done anything wrong. I started to walk faster; he followed! I ran toward the door. From nowhere, two other officers appeared right in front of me.

"Just stop right there sir!" the one on the left shouted.

Then out of the corner of my eye, I saw another guy, not in uniform, waving at the policemen. It was Spike.

"It's okay Matthew, he's one of mine!" he shouted.

The policemen looked at him, nodded, and walked away.

"You cunt!" He laughed. "What the fuck is wrong with you? The fucking war is over, you tit!" He grabbed me and we hugged like long lost brothers.

Later we parked in front of the Europa Hotel. That had changed just as much as the airport. Everywhere looked clean and modern. It seemed bizarre. We went straight into the bar. Funnily enough, I noticed that war correspondent sitting in the bar on her own. What was her name? Kate Ade. I looked at her and then at Spike.

"See? Not everything has changed," I said.

We both burst out laughing. Kate Ade looked at us as though we had just landed from Mars, not impressed, I suppose.

It was around 2300 hours (11 P.M.) when Spike decided that it was time to eat. Good thing really, as I hadn't even had any lunch. Nothing special, I insisted, as we walked along the road to the local Chinese. *Hmm, I remember this place,* I thought to myself.

"Hey, I expect you remember this place," Spike blurted.

Just shows that we all share some memories, usually of things that we don't really want to remember.

"Yes, this is the first place I bumped into Spook," I explained.

"I know," he smirked, and we walked in.

The restaurant hadn't changed much, apart from the walls were covered in some kind of red velvet wallpaper. It looked really cheap. We walked to the reception desk, where a rather pretty young Chinese looking girl stood smiling.

"We've booked," Spike said.

"Yes, Mr. Spike, the others are already at your table," she explained.

"What others?" I asked, feeling like this was a bit of a setup. Just for a minute I began to get that old panicky feeling in the base of my stomach. It's like a fluttering feeling. I suppose most people have experienced it at some point or other. It's strange, but keeps you vigilant.

We walked into the restaurant between the two level rows of tables. Each table had four chairs around it. Everything was red, even the candles.

"Looks like they are expecting the Labour party in here tonight," I said.

"Bit more than the Labour party," Spike giggled.

We walked up about five steps and around into a separate room, through some red curtains and into a large dining room. The lights were quite dim, and there was a large round table in the middle of the room. The room was all in red! Fifteen people sat around the table, with just two spaces at the other end of the room. As soon as the people sitting around the table realized we had entered the room, they all stood up and started moving toward us. At this point I realized what was going on!

"For fuck's sake," I exclaimed. "John! (Also earlier referred to as 'The RSM' or Jossie) What the fuck are you doing here?"

"Waiting for you! You cunt!" he replied in his old, well-mannered Scottish accent.

I saw Spook, Rick, and quite a few others also standing around the table.

"Welcome home!" laughed Spike.

We all took our seats and gossiped and bantered for the next fifteen minutes.

The food had already been ordered. I suppose that was the good thing about a bunch of guys like us–nobody really disliked anything, so anybody could order without worrying about what to order.

I noticed Tommo sat a couple of seats down from me. "What happened to you mate? Last time I saw you, you were a PTI in the Artillery."

"Yeah, I volunteered for DET, where I met Spook and everyone, then went onto the Regiment (22 SAS)."

There was suddenly hissing and whispers of "Tosser" and lots of laughing. See the thing with the Regiment–We always felt that they were an okay bunch of guys. They trained hard and were really good at achieving things that intelligent people had prearranged for them, however, look at stories like Bravo 20, etc. Some great guys involved, some real heroes made to look like tossers by their own mates! I mean why write a book that you know will piss off your former colleagues? For money? I have heard the stories told about Sgt. Phillips and I think I know the truth. The bloke who wrote the book, and made him out to be inadequate, should have a serious chat with himself. Phillips was a great guy; he achieved great things, and thus should be remembered as such.

We tended to look at the regiment as a group of good guys, slowly but surely building on their reputation with the public. I wouldn't argue that they were good, just maybe a little short sighted. Tommo didn't agree, not surprisingly, thus a somewhat ludicrous debate whilst we tucked into our Chinese.

"Anyway," I said, "What are we all doing here? If it's a reunion, it's a little strange."

The room went silent.

"Okay, Topper, as you ask so bluntly, maybe it's time we let you into a little secret," explained Spike. "We belong to an organization that was formed just over five years ago. It was set up primarily to deal with the issues unable to be resolved by the Army, RUC (or PSNI), or anyone else for that matter."

“I thought we had organizations for that purpose, those affiliated with MI6?” I asked.

“Well, yes and then again, no,” he answered. “Topper, the problem has always been the same; some of the fuckers here in Northern Ireland will never get their just desserts. We all know that, including our most loyal government!” There were a few sniggers around the room.

“Therefore, we are the current generation that is responsible, from a variety of backgrounds, for ensuring processes of law here in Northern Ireland are able to reach their ultimate conclusion.”

I sat for a while and looked at him. I then looked around the room at the others. Everyone was quiet. “I’m not sure I understand,” I lied.

“Well, may I suggest that we eat and get pissed tonight, then spend some time tomorrow going through the detail? If you like what you see and hear, then we can all talk further. If not, then no harm done. Oh and we know we can trust you to keep a secret.”

More sniggering.

Strange, even some of the guys that I thought I knew well turned out to be complete strangers. I mean, not one of them had trusted me enough to tell me about all this. But, I suppose in life, when you each go your separate ways, regardless what you have been through together, things change, people change and thus, so does their focus!

Chapter Twenty

I woke with a cracking hangover. Spike was already up. I think we were in one of his friend's houses, or such was the impression. He stood in the bathroom shaving. I could see him through the doorway of the bedroom in which I had been sleeping. The door was ajar.

He was humming to himself, seemed quite happy.

I smiled to myself. God this felt familiar. "So Spike, what's the plan?" I asked.

"Get your fat arse out of bed and I'll talk you through it," he replied.

About an hour later, I sat facing a full cooked English breakfast, kindly provided by a rather young looking girl, with dark hair, slim, and very pretty. We were in the kitchen of the house. I was amazed. I remember being driven here last night, but I didn't realize we had left the city. I must have fallen asleep.

The view out of the kitchen window was great. You could see the Black Mountains and as far back as I can remember, for the first time in my experience, the weather was great. But in fairness, my experiences in Belfast had been usually kept strictly to night times.

"Hi, thanks very much for this. It looks great," I said to the young lady, as nicely as I knew how.

"Right," was her brief reply.

Her accent was strange. She only said one word, but such a strange accent.

I looked across at Spike, just as he was stuffing a piece of bread in his mouth.

"What?" he mumbled, extending his hands out to each side.

I waited till she left the room. "Who is she?" I asked.

He laughed and had to pull some of the bread back out of his mouth so as not to choke on it.

"She looks familiar?" he asked.

"I don't know. There is something about her."

He laughed again. The young girl came back into the room.

"Tell Topper who you are," he told her, smiling.

She turned and looked straight at me. "My mother is Denise; I believe she is a friend of yours."

Well, fuck me again. This was Harvey's daughter. Oh my God.

"Denise will be here shortly, she's just gone for the papers," explained Spike.

"Think you better explain," I said.

"This is her house, this is her daughter. We are her friends. What else is there to know?"

I felt a little angry. Why were we in her house? Her husband was my partner; he died working with me, why? And there she was.

"For fuck's sake, you've put more weight on," she said, in her broad northern accent. We hugged and she cried. We sat down and she told me everything that had happened since I left.

She explained to her daughter that she had tried to get in touch after I left the hospital, but they didn't want to release my new identity. She had named her daughter Alex, as I had named my first son Alexander. She went on to explain that the services had gone through the death of Harvey with her in loads of detail, and gave her all the assurances that she needed that it wasn't our fault.

After a few months, she had become embroiled working for an RUC unit specializing in entrapping members of the IRA, either for blackmailing opportunities or for extraction. Extraction meant simply removing them from the arena, any way possible. You see, all those years of the public being led to believe that the IRA were all bad and naturally we, the British (including the RUC), were all good, wasn't necessarily always true. I know it comes as a shock (ha-ha).

She explained in detail about how she had become this great asset in the fight against terrorism in Northern Ireland and indeed the devastating effect the death of her husband had had on her and her relationship with her family. I must admit, I was amazed. I was starting to believe that it wasn't just me that had experienced something difficult in life and indeed, it wasn't just me that had suffered because of the death of a colleague.

We talked for some time.

It must have been lunchtime when Spike walked back into the room. I hadn't even noticed him leave. I asked when I was last here why she hadn't acknowledged all these things, and why she had pretended not to know who Spook was. She laughed.

"Because you admitted you knew who Spook was."

"Okay, it's becoming really boring now. Why don't you two just have a shag and get it out of your systems for fuck's sake!" He laughed.

"I forgot you were a comedian, Spike," I replied.

"I have a few things I need to discuss with you, Topper. In particular the matters that were touched upon last night. Time is short and I know you two have a lot to talk about, but this is urgent. I need to be clear before I see the others."

I looked at him, confused.

"You wanted to know what we were all doing here, right?"

"Yes," I replied.

"Well, get your shit together and we'll go for a drive and I'll explain on the way," he said.

Within minutes we were in the car, heading up into the Black Mountains.

"Where we going?" I asked.

"Nowhere yet, just driving around making sure we are going alone."

"Oh," I mumbled, feeling a little out of touch.

We drove in numerous directions, until finally we were heading toward Newry. We travelled along the A1 past some memorable places, indeed some places that the IRA would never have guessed we had bases. We passed Dromore, Loughbrickland down as far as Newry. The place hadn't changed half as much as Belfast. Then again, I suppose it hadn't received the television coverage and therefore didn't get the same investment. Shame really, nice place.

We then headed to a small place called Kilcurry.

Now this place I remembered very well. The locals had been oblivious to what had gone on right under their noses.

"Enlighten me, Spike. What on earth would we be doing here?" I asked.

"Thought you would like this place. Just the place for you meet an old friend of yours," he replied. Although he sounded confident, there was an element of doubt in his voice.

We drove to a small white house just on the outskirts of the village. There were four cars parked outside, which in itself looked suspicious in this area. Either someone had died, or the naughty boys' brigade was in town. I was soon to find out which!

The door opened before we reached it and a large built guy raised his hand in a gesture to stop. We did. He beckoned Spike forward and spoke quietly to him. He asked him to turn around whilst he searched him. Once happy, he beckoned me forward.

"Turn around and face the door please," he said in a local accent. He searched me. Again once happy, he ushered us both past the door and left into what seemed an awfully small living room.

I couldn't believe my eyes. Martin McGuiness! I still hated him, and I'm sure he knew that from the minute I set eyes on him

"Fuck this, Spike. Whatever it is, I don't want to be part of it!"

I started to push past the big guy. He put out his hand as if he were going to try and stop me. I grabbed his wrist and, in the flicker of an eye, twisted his wrist completely around until he was screaming for me to stop. I kicked out with my right foot into the back of his knees and he fell to the ground.

"All right, Topper, that's enough!" shouted Spike. "We are here to talk."

"I have no interest in talking to that prick," I said.

McGuiness didn't move. He just stood and watched. I could hear some shuffling going on in another room, so I assumed we were obviously not alone in the house.

"Listen to me, mister," McGuiness finally said. "I'm here to do you a favor. You're obviously new to all this, so why don't you listen before jumping to stupid conclusions?"

I loosened my grip on the big guy's wrist. He rubbed it for a short while before getting back up on his feet. McGuiness gestured for him leave the room.

"We have been working with each other for some time now. We realized some time ago that this war wasn't going anywhere. That's why we contacted your government and made the peace deal a reality. You will be surprised to hear that it isn't us who are continuing all the trouble. It's either the real IRA or a few idiots that can't see the wood for the trees. We do, however, still have access to all sorts of ammunition and guns that your government would like to display on the television to give the British people the satisfaction of believing that they have won the war. That's fine by us, but you get nothing for nothing in this world, as I'm sure you know. Now Spike tells me you're the man who can sort a lot of problems out for us, that's us both, not just us Sinn Fein. If that's really the case, we will show our gratitude in a way that you wouldn't think possible."

"You mean by double crossing us," I rudely interrupted.

"Listen, mister, we all have memories, mainly bad ones. I even remember you stopping me at a check point years ago and making me look a cunt in front of your checkpoint people. I had plenty of opportunity of trying to find you and getting you done, but I didn't. You know why?"

I nodded my head

"Because I knew how you felt. We were bastards, and had to be. You can't imagine how pressured it was to be a bastard all of the time. The moment anyone thought you were softening, you were dead. So mister, let's talk about now, rather than fuck about worrying about what happened in the past!"

I just stared at him for a while. "Okay, what have you got in mind?" I asked.

We discussed a number of issues over the next couple of hours, including Sinn Fein's problem people, the ever-changing face of the UFF and all the others. Most importantly, how difficult it was for all sides to deal with people who wanted the conflict to continue and thus were motivating hatred between the two peoples again. The conclusion was inevitable.

Chapter Twenty-One

I had a lot to think about. We arrived back at Denise's house after dark. My head was cabbaged. She made us egg, chips, and beans.

"You're quiet," she suggested inquisitively.

"I need to think," I mumbled.

"Good," she exclaimed, as she wandered off into another room.

I was conscious of Spike staring at me. "Will you fuck off, please?" I asked.

"What is there to think about," he asked.

"A fucking lot! In case you hadn't noticed, I have a new life in the UK. I have a job, a house, and I'm not getting any younger. You just expect me to drop everything and become part of the Northern Ireland's solution to 'After Terrorism'? Trust me, it isn't that easy for me."

"No, no, no. I don't expect you to give up anything. I don't even expect you to work for me! I want to work for you, as do the others! It was the fucking IRA who suggested you were the ideal person for this role. You think that prick would have gone out of his way to meet anyone else? For fuck sake, Topper, if I wanted a recruitment consultant, I wouldn't have picked Martin fucking McGuiness." He went on to explain that we had a number of houses at our disposal, as many firearms as we would need, in fact, almost anything required to help eliminate the problem. The problem was people!

We all had our normal jobs in the UK. It would either be a prearranged party or a social visit. The RUC/PSNI wouldn't bother us; the only danger would be the people we had to get rid of. Then it clicked. The police at the airport were there to make sure we arrived safely and nobody bothered us. Fuck, this little scheme was clever and involved all kinds of people.

"What British government officials are involved?" I asked.

"You can meet them tomorrow," he replied, smiling.

I'm not sure if I was amazed or horrified. Either way, I didn't feel comfortable, more confused. If I'm honest, it was all starting to bring back feelings and emotions that I wasn't really ready to play with.

We went to a local pub and had a pub dinner. I can't even remember what it was. Mind you, most pub grub around the area is best forgotten, and easily done after a few pints. We got back to the house just after midnight. We had talked about all sorts through the night, but nothing really specific. Spike certainly wasn't smiling anymore. He could tell I wasn't happy.

We sat in the living room, bit of a dreary room. It had the funny squiggly seventies wallpaper, with green bits, which I suppose were supposed to be flowers. The cream suite matched the other predominant color in the paper. There was a large cupboard, known as a shrank, with lots of photos, medals, and trophies on it. It reminded me of our house when we lived in Germany many years ago. The telly was a small portable thing that looked like one of those things you would expect to find in a skip. The house was warm though. I suppose that was the main thing.

"Another beer, Top?" asked Spike.

I sort of hummed in acknowledgment.

He went into the kitchen. I heard him talking to someone, but couldn't make out what he was saying. The voices seemed to get a bit heated, so I decided to go and find out who was there. It was Denise.

"What are you two arguing about?" I asked.

"You," replied Denise, looking sharply at Spike. "I was explaining to the apparent uneducated how difficult it must be for you after all this time to feel as though you're being dragged back into things."

"Come on, Top," interrupted Spike. "You know it isn't like that, don't you?"

"To be quite honest, Spike, I'm not sure what it's like at the moment. You must admit, it's a lot to take in, in just over twenty-four hours."

He looked at me thoughtfully for a moment. "Yes, I suppose you're right. I have rushed things a little."

"Listen," I said quite abruptly. "It's me. After all the shit we went through, even meeting Denise again, and all the lads, it's a lot for me to deal with. Just give me a bit of time to get my head around it all and I'll probably be okay."

He smiled again. "Okay, Top. You're right. You get your head down here and I'll go see the lads. I'll tell them you're knackered and need a bit of time. Maybe we can all meet up for lunch tomorrow, eh?"

"Sounds great," I answered.

We all hugged and Spike grabbed his jacket and went out the front door.

"You all right?" asked Denise.

"Yes, it's all just a bit of a shock. Life has moved on since those days and I never imagined ever getting involved again. I spent some horrible nights in that psycho ward and I never actually knew how badly it had affected me until this afternoon."

"I know what you mean," she replied.

I must have looked at her strangely.

"Oh, trust me, I do!"

I sat back down on the couch in front of the little TV. It was switched off.

She started to tell me all about the time after Harvey had died how she had struggled to accept that it wasn't anyone's fault, although the service went to great lengths to prove otherwise. Once she had accepted it was one of those things, all she wanted to do was avenge his death. She even worked for a short period of time with the UVF. She had helped set up two IRA men who thought they were going to her house for a good night. They certainly got it good, but not what they had been expecting.

The RUC had picked her up whilst she was carrying a 9mm Smith and Western in her handbag. Apparently they only let her off because the service had intervened. Not happy with that, she volunteered to help them.

I was amazed. At least I was forced to leave when I had become a liability, she experienced the opposite. They used her for their own convenience.

She was good. She knew everyone that she needed to know. She could provide enough plans to enable a successful kidnap or termination. No wonder they had been quite happy to leave her with me for the night. I was trying not to confuse her with the old Denise that I had known.

Anyway, it was getting to the time where I wasn't really bothered. I was starting to relax. My mind was starting to waken. I knew if I went to sleep now, I would be back in my dreams.

"You look tired," she said, stroking my forehead.

"Time for the specialist moves. The ones that can maybe instigated by a woman." Little did she know, I was already convinced!

But, I was a man and a man had needs. So, I would play along and well. I suppose a shag is a shag.

I woke up about six. It was light. It was quiet and I couldn't hear any cars outside. Denise was asleep on the floor with blanket over her top torso. Her arse was sticking out of the blanket. I laughed!

"What the fuck are you laughing at," she demanded to know.

"Your arse is sticking out of the blanket," I said.

"Oh, fuck off!" she replied, rolling over so she could see me.

"Well, come on, get up, and make my breakfast, bitch!" I laughed. "You're supposed to be convincing me to join your band of merry men."

"You bastard! When did you decide?" she asked.

"Just before you started sucking my dick!" I continued, laughing.

"Oh. well, I wanted to fuck you anyway," she mumbled. She got up, kissed me on the forehead, and wandered off into the kitchen. She wrapped the blanket around her shoulders.

We walked after breakfast. She kept saying, "Don't look so paranoid, nobody here knows you. It's fine."

I suppose old habits die hard.

When we returned to the house, Spike, Jossie, and Spook were waiting outside in a blue Datsun Cherry.

"Tell you what, Spike, I always said you would find the ideal car. This job must pay you well!"

Everybody laughed.

We went into the kitchen. Spike looked at me and started to apologize for being so forward, apparently some of the others had said he should have taken the slow approach, but as ever he didn't listen.

"Don't worry, I'm convinced," I said, butting in. "But I need to go home and sort a few things out. I also need a proper briefing and an understanding of what is expected and what we get out of it."

"Fuck, Topper! Last night I thought you were going home to never come back! What changed your mind?" asked Spike.

"I did!" is all I answered.

Spook grabbed hold of me and hugged me; Jossie just patted me on the back. He was never an emotional type of guy, but hey, what the heck, he could shoot straight and wouldn't run off and leave you when you needed him.

I got my brief and I must say, to this day I am amazed how clever people can be...particularly people in authority.

I flew back on the last flight into Liverpool. My girlfriend picked me up from the airport. Funnily enough, her dad was a great supporter of a united Ireland, but had always said to her that when I was ready to tell her about my army career, she should never be judgmental, as it is all a lot more complicated than it seems. Great words from a guy who turned out to be a right tosser!

Two years later he was found to be shagging his secretary and got her pregnant. He did the honorable thing and dumped his wife and moved in with the secretary. He sold his business for a few million and gave his wife nothing! Nice.

Chapter Twenty-Two

I was at a stage of my life when I was actually considering becoming normal. I had been through quite a bit and I had, on occasion, considered calming down. You know, buy a house, move in with someone, stick to a normal job, on normal pay. Finish work and go home to the misses. It makes me laugh even now, but I was considering it.

The public transport place I was working for was being sold to one of the bigger national operators. I had no inclination whatsoever to work for them. There were and probably still are all sorts of illegal insider deals going on between the Public Transport Authority and the so-called private operators.

I remember that guy called Scales taking all sorts of cash bungs from both my old friend, or my girlfriend's dad, and ourselves. I remember all the meetings between them and the police, discussing the best way to squander the public's money.

It's amazing how much money–public money, Merseyside people's money–is squandered on just one organization. The amount of people surplus to requirement or even in jobs that don't really require doing, or in roles which would be better served by a temp is amazing. The problem is, if ever an audit were carried out, their auditors would be briefed to ensure that the appropriate words were used to pacify the public.

See, we don't live in a democracy at all. Because the government tell you it's one, doesn't mean that it is. Yes, we vote. We vote for the person who lies the best, or the most. Once elected, they don't give a stuff what we as individuals think, they just play homage to their leader, who again, doesn't give a stuff about what goes on in your area. Take this Gordon Brown fellow. I cannot believe that any normal thinking English man would want to be represented by him. That doesn't mean I think he is a bad man; no, I just think his image is appalling, his views are archaic, and he is just another of what we have endured for years. Anyway, I left the transport company and set up a private security company.

It was great fun. We directly associated ourselves with another company based in Woking. We focused on basic security services to dock authority. I remember when there was all that hassle over the importation of GM grain from America. We worked with a company on the Liverpool docks and the port police in stopping the environmentalists causing disruption to the imports. We used to patrol the port in power boats, during the day and night, making sure that these buggers never got in.

On one occasion, we advised the company that they should maintain high levels of manning for the duration of the risk. They declined and reduced the levels considerably. Inevitably, they came. They had hired a couple of vans and bought a couple of ferry tickets for Norse Irish Ferries, who were based next door.

They showed their tickets to the port police at the main gates, who let them into the docks. They drove straight at the guys looking after the gates to the company we were responsible for.

They leapt out from the vans. There must have been fifty of them squashed into these two vans.

Someone cut the brake pipes on the vans, so they couldn't be moved. They then ran all over the place. Most of them chained themselves to stupid places that would obviously cause disruption. Others, obviously the better trained ones, climbed one hundred-foot gantries and chained themselves up there. The rest, who were obviously qualified climbers, hung from the gantries in those small mountaineering tents.

It took us most of the day to cut through the chain and get the majority out. But the ones hanging from tents were obviously there to stay, or so they thought.

During the night, once everybody had gone home and left us to it, I told the boys that every twenty minutes or so, they should get above the tents and cause a racket, not let them get any sleep. Well, typical ex-servicemen. They were not just making a racket, they were pissing on the tents, throwing things at them; well, you can imagine.

A port police car pulled up at the gates. It was the duty sergeant.

"Greenpeace safety officer has been on the phone, saying that their guys feel that they are being put at risk by the antics of the security men," he said.

"That's crap; nobody has been any where near them. If anything, it's windy and the grain and things are being blown all over the place. Maybe it's that," I replied.

"That will do for me," said the sergeant, as he walked back to his car laughing.

The disruption carried on until around three in the morning. Then we let them sleep. Dangling just below their tents were small bags, which contained their water, food, and essentials.

About 0330 hours, I and one of the others abseiled down to each tent and removed all their food and water. We returned to the roof, all done by 0400 hours. At 0415 hours, the boys started again. Funnily enough, by 0800 hours, we had received a call from the police saying that the guys in their tents wanted to come down. Amazing, eh!

The thing is, these organizations or the proper ones have their own health and safety laws, and no matter what, if you do not have the appropriate food and water, you cannot stay in one of those elevated tents for very long.

It was great fun. Well, we thought so!

Chapter Twenty-Three

I returned to NI a couple of times and yes, we did become pretty proficient at what we needed to do. We only took out people that were either being hunted by the services for murder, or people that would eventually stand in the way of peaceful resolutions to the future of NI–only, of course, on the basis that it was going to remain British.

Why not McGuiness and his cronies, I hear you question?

To be quite honest, both McGuiness and Adams–Adams actually being the underdog, and always has been–were no longer in a position to be active service members of the IRA. They could always be manipulated by the British government to help in the fight to provide stability. See, their sole aim in life was to fight for a united Ireland. This has not happened. Thus, in effect, their fight, or struggle as they like to call it, has effectively been a waste of time and life.

If they become active politicians, fighting for a united Ireland through political channels, they are seen to be still fighting and not to have lost. Regardless…they lost. All those killings on their behalf were fruitless. They are now, whether they like it or not...British!

They form part of a coalition Northern Irish Government, or assembly. This assembly is governed by the British Government….They are British.

CHAPTER TWENTY-FOUR

Back in the hospital, I was still trying to work out what the smell was. Then it came to me–the smell of hospitals, the cleanliness, the chemicals they use to kill bacteria (although not very successfully nowadays), the hissing of leaking oxygen from those plug-in inlets in the walls by the beds. I was in hospital.

I remember now what happened. I was employed by a large landowner's estate manager to sort out their estate security problems. The estate is huge, however, in one of the northern areas notorious for trouble. It has a walled section of the estate, measuring about twenty-five hundred acres. Within the walls is a safari park, covering about five hundred acres. It has the usual safari park attractions, with the usual safari park animals, including lions, tigers, etc.

The estate houses a fabulous hall, which is also within the walls. The estate has existed since the fourteenth century. It is engulfed with some fantastic history and I deemed it a privilege to work there. Previously, the hall had been rented out to the police who had made a right pig's ear of the place. Luckily for the future generations in the area, the new landowner refurbished the whole hall and brought it back to its original grandeur, with the professional guidance of his wife, of course. The place is now used for functions, like weddings, meetings, etc., very popular. With the location of the estate, the obvious local problems exist.

When I first arrived, I noticed quite a few local lads and girls wandering around, just being lads and girls really, however, with the odd exception of arson, theft and criminal damage. We often came across drug paraphernalia around the quiet zones. See, it was a great place for addicts to go after they had scored. Before we arrived, it was highly unlikely that anyone would stumble across them.

The main concern was burglary. Whilst for the duration of my stay there, we only ever experienced two inside the walls; locally, the farms, which also were deemed part of the estate, were burgled quite regularly.

The family–the landowner and his wife and children–were often at home and hence it was always important to keep the locals at a distance. Anyway, I think we had been working there about a month. The estate manager called me to his office. He told me about a large function they were planning, a charity dinner in support of the NSPCC.

I think the landowner's wife was a patron, or one of the charity's great supporters. She was a great supporter of quiet a few charities. I think the most popular is the Imagine Appeal. That's the charity that helps fund Alder Hey Hospital in Liverpool. What a fabulous place; just for kids.

This NSPCC dinner was to have some celebrity guests. One of the guests was going to be Prince Andrew.

I suppose most people would have been in awe; after all he is a member of the royal family. It meant we had a few extra arrangements to make. The function would take place in a huge marquee on the rear lawns of the hall. The alcohol was to be delivered to the marquee about two days prior, and thus we needed to ensure that we had security within the marquee from the outset of its delivery, until the function itself. After that, it would become someone else's problem.

We made all the necessary arrangements, and, as planned, once the alcohol was delivered, two security staff were present in the marquee for the duration. Two days prior to the event the estate manager called me to his office. He explained to me that Prince Andrew's personal protection officer would be arriving late in the evening in order to look at the marquee and assess the security situation. I decided that because it was us who were on show to this guy, and, of course, he would try and find something wrong even if to merely justify his existence, we would, that's Jason and I, be around.

I think it was about nineish in the evening; it was quiet. The security guards were in the marquee, all under control. We went in to the estate club for an orange juice.

The estate club was one of those typical places that had been opened for the staff and residents on site to enjoy. After a few pints, nobody really minded if you drove home. Well, you weren't likely to drive on a public highway. The only agreement was that if you ran over a sheep or something, you should admit it and pay for it at market price. However, it had become more difficult over the years, as the landowner had started renting the hall out for weddings and functions. The club was situated almost next door. It would be difficult to explain away someone driving home from the club pissed, and running over a wedding guest. But then, I suppose it wouldn't be hard to get rid of the body in an estate that contained a safari park.

Estates of this nature usually suffer when it comes to modernization and change. Most staff are long serving, and as with some corps of the army, resent change. It's the age-old, "it's not broke, it has always worked this way, why fix it?"

I remember one of the Gamekeepers stopping me and saying, "Don't know why we have security, I've been here for forty years, and we have never had security."

I couldn't even think of where to start, so I didn't.

The club was a throw back from years gone by. Remember, I referred to that pub earlier, in the film "American Werewolf in London." Well, that says it all. People went there for gossip, the same people all the time; same stories, but sometimes amended a little to make them sound more exciting.

Often I walked in there and the conversation stopped.

The barman, as with all clubs, was the greatest instigator of rumors. He always nice to your face, but would never disagree with anyone who called you names. I don't just mean me, I mean everybody. Funnily enough, in later years, he was the one suspected to be the reason the place never made profit. Oh, the prices. You would expect that on a private estate, the prices would be relatively low, some agreement with the brewery, or his ability to obtain reduced beer costs through the hall. No, in fact a pint of lager was generally about 25p more than in the local pubs.

He and his fellow barperson paid themselves cash £100 every week that they worked. Strange place.

We popped in and ordered a couple of drinks. Mobile phone reception in the club was terrible, so I had to keep going outside to take calls from friends and security calls alike. About ten, we left the club and decided to have a drive around the estate. We drove to one of the gates, one of the main electronically controlled gates, which led into the local village. We exited the gates, and sat in the dark adjacent to the woods in view of the gates. We listened for anyone stalking around in the woods outside. We sat there for approximately five minutes when two cars came screaming along the main road towards us.

I got out and walked toward to electronic access system where the first of the cars had stopped. The access system is situated on the pavement near the gate. The second car stopped opposite the lane leading into the village. I remember thinking, *this looked like the perfect set up for a hit.*

The first car drove to me and the driver's side window was open. The driver called out, "Police. Open the gate."

I looked inside and there were three of them, all carrying firearms.

I turned and unlocked the gate. The driver drove through, and once through, the second car approached. It was a green Aston Martin. I could see that the driver was Prince Andrew.

Oh, shit, I thought. I was sure he wasn't supposed to be coming until the following evening.

They drove in through the gates and up toward the landowner's house. We went back to the marquee to see if his equerry had been. He hadn't.

We decided to patrol around the estate to make sure things were in order. After driving around for a while, we drove up the road leading to the landowner's house. This road runs alongside the main carriageway inside the estate, but also goes onto the hall and allows you to turn toward the main lake inside the estate. The lake is fabulous. It's named after a statue, which overlooks the whole of the estate. Years and years ago, the statue was erected above the lake, which I think was found whilst digging the lake out. The statue doesn't really have a title, but is a statue of a white man.

We turned toward the lake. As we crossed a cattle grid, to our left was an open field, which led back to the gate I referred to earlier. Jason shouted for me to stop.

"What's wrong," I asked.

"I'm sure I saw two people in the field," he replied.

I spun the car around, and as I was now nearest the fence, I took the lamp. I shone it across the field. Sure enough, I could see someone running in the opposite direction from us, towards the road we had driven up, through the trees. This wasn't really anything unusual; it just felt it because of the misinformation regarding the visit.

We would often come across people in the estate, either looking for rabbits, or seeing what residents had left in their gardens worth stealing. As usual, we chased them. It was pretty usual that, as we got close to whoever they were, they would jump over the wall and disappear into the night. There wasn't a lot we could do after that point, as they had only been trespassing, which is not a criminal offense, thus the police didn't really want to be bothered with it. Not that I blame them, what with everyday shootings and massive amounts of drug incidents they are having to cope with. I'm sure they have more important things to be getting on with.

We drove down to the community college, which is situated within the estate walls. It's a college where youngsters learn about horticulture or chainsaw operations; particularly well worthwhile place, even though frequented by many of the young gentlemen we have chased off from the estate. Personally, I would rather they were sent off into the army, learned the same things, but learned some discipline along the way.

We had many run-ins with the youngsters that attend this college. Either they harassed the sheep, or they wandered into places they shouldn't, or they sat around smoking pot. You drove up a tarmac drive, large enough for a single vehicle one way only.

On the right, on the way up was an elongated car park, only wide enough for cars to park one deep, side by side. Opposite that was a small pine wood, mostly chopped to bits where the kids had been learning to use chainsaws. Further up, you had a choice of taking a sharp left turn onto the main car park, which backed onto the estate exterior wall. The car park was probably about eighty feet long by forty feet wide. It was shale I think. The wall was around six feet high and made of red sandstone. It looked like it would take hundreds of men hundreds of years to build.

The alternative was to turn right onto the forecourt of the college building. This was a completely enclosed courtyard with the actual college on one side and a stable, game room, and a couple of garages on the other. Neither area had any form of lighting, so you can imagine how dark it was at night. The car park on the left had two large skips on it, which appeared to be quite full; those great big yellow things and as usual, the rubbish appeared to be almost overflowing. We stopped the vehicle between the main car park and the college forecourt. It was pretty dark. I looked at Jason.

"You check the forecourt, I'll check the car park," I said. I didn't feel at all worried as I really expected this to have been a couple of idiots that had jumped back over the wall.

Jason walked off into the forecourt.

I walked toward the skips; they were on my right side. I stood for a second in the darkness. It was so peaceful. I turned to my left about to continue walking. I heard a noise from behind me. I spun around and, as I did, I felt an almighty thud on the side of my head. I remember seeing someone standing at the side of the skip with what appeared to be a long metal object in his hand. He was short but quite stocky. I immediately grabbed toward him, punching and grabbing. I felt as though I couldn't move fast enough to keep up with my thoughts. It was as though I had withdrawn back inside my own head. I felt distant. It felt more like a film that I was trying to participate in, but it was too far away.

I remember hearing a buzzing noise and the outer sides of my vision started to go black.

Chapter Twenty-Five

It must have only been a few seconds, or minutes at the most. I then remember hearing a shot! Quite distinctively, a shot! I tried to get up; I was trying to figure out what was happening. I looked to my left, toward where we had parked the vehicle. I could see Jason getting up off the floor.

Oh, shit, he's been shot, I thought. I couldn't get up. I turned to my right and saw someone climbing the wall; he rested his stomach on the top and seemed to vault over.

Then Jason was stood over me. He was panic stricken. "Oh fuck, Tony, they shot you!" he shouted at me.

I tried to get up again, but I couldn't. It was weird, I felt drunk. I certainly didn't feel as though I had been shot! I heard Jason phone for the police. Funny though, I started to feel quite relaxed. I felt as though my senses were starting to return. I wasn't worried at all.

Jason stayed over me for ages, it seemed, trying to convince me that all was okay. I remember him calling for the police and an ambulance again and they said the police had gone to the wrong estate and the ambulance can't come to us until the police arrived. Bloody police policy! Apparently it took over forty minutes for the police to arrive....lucky I hadn't been shot in the head!

When they arrived, it was quite amusing. The Armed Response Teams came running in like one of those American SWAT teams. I must say though, they did look quite impressive! One of them dressed my injury with one of those military field dressings; I was even more impressed. Then the 'out of touchers' arrived. You know, the senior guys who have no police experience, no life experience, but went to university, and thus qualify to be senior police officers...and we wonder where it all went wrong.

I could see the police helicopter overhead. God, there were quite a few police around by the time I was taken away.

We arrived at the local hospital, about five miles from where the incident happened. It's strange though, when you get brought in with police escorts and under armed escort, everyone seems to look at you as though you some kind of criminal.

We were put into a side room. They posted a guard outside the room, a 5'6" female, who looked like her body armor and her gun…oh, I've already said that.

Later, they took me upstairs, still swamped by the police. I remember two of them in particular, real tossers. One of them actually told me he was an ex-squaddie. They were trying some good-cop-bad-cop shit with me. It was hilarious. I remember them asking me if could they search my house. I mean, what the fuck do they want to search my house for? I thought it was me that was the victim. Then I saw a face that made it all click into place.

Whilst looking after public transport security, I remember a Superintendent Ted Greenwell, fantastic bloke who was responsible for South Liverpool. Old style copper, but he had a real bimbo of a detective inspector sent to run his CID section. The DCI was suspended for some non-entity at the time, although later reinstated and flew through the ranks. She seemed to disagree with everything we wanted to do, quoting different aspects of the law, etc.

I remember all that time ago thinking that if this was a vision of future policing, then boy, are we in trouble…and low and behold, it's true. I think she's a superintendent somewhere now.

Anyway, she was the duty person responsible for dealing with my case. I was treated disgracefully. I remember even when I was going down to be operated on, the two CID muppets threatening to get a search warrant to search my house. For fuck's sake, as though I cared. I must admit though, at that point, if I hadn't felt so unwell, I probably would have put them both in hospital. You know the type, they hide behind the badge. Yet in reality, very low esteem excuses for men. They probably never made it in the army, probably the ones who complained about bullying! Wankers! They did get a search warrant. You see, magistrates are selected on the basis that most magistrates have no experience of anything bad. Therefore, they will never really be able to make an accurate or independent judgement on things.

So, two police officers turn up on your door early hours of the morning with stories of attempted murder and dropping names such as Prince Andrew, etc., yes, they will sign the warrant. The system sucks.

The house was searched and everything they took, they subsequently had to return. The lads on the search were actually good guys, mind. They were respectful and discreet. Probably knew that the stupid bitch was making a big mistake. I mean, for fuck's sake, my brother is a copper.

In the hospital, they cut open my arm, cleaned the wound, and stitched me back together. On the ward I was like a leper. Nobody spoke to me, the nurses never really had any time for me, and I never once saw a doctor. They discharged me at my request and they never even changed my dressing, which, trust me, I had murder trying to get off a few days later.

Let me tell you the worst thing though. Because they couldn't find an immediate answer to what had gone on, the then-chief constable and allegedly others agreed that "They had probably been messing around with a hand gun and it had gone off!"

See, I have it on good authority that this was the conclusion. I even remember the press release that they gave out: *A 38-year-old game keeper was shot last night whilst trying to apprehend poachers.*

I was not 38 and certainly not a gamekeeper.

Only one person came to see me from the estate; everyone else distanced themselves. One of the gamekeepers at the time, Big N, had a son called Tom. The young lad came to the house with a bottle of scotch and wished me all the best and a speedy recovery. Do you know, to this day, I like the guy? No get well cards, nothing. See, what happens with people like these is, they employ you to do a job. If you die, hurt yourself, or do anything else that may bring them into the public eye, everybody seems to distance themselves from you.

Anyway, that's in the past.

My arm healed well. I was quickly back to good health. Three years later I received a call from the police. They had found the gun; they knew who had done the shooting, but were doubtful that they would have enough evidence to prosecute. They wanted to know if I would still be willing to go to court.

I told them, if they were to give me the address and name of the person, I could save the taxpayer thousands of pounds. Funnily enough, I never heard anything after that.

I received a call from Spike.

"Hi mate, rumor has it you've been playing with the bad boys in Liverpool!"

"Very fucking funny," I replied, listening to his laughter in the background.

"Well, we have an enormous job come through, which I think you are perfect for."

And on it goes!

We have all suffered difficulties in life!

Some through stresses at work, others domestic pressures, others just general day-to-day life!

This book gives an insight into another military organization that, unlike the now seemingly exposed SAS, will always remain secret.

From the Falklands to Colombia, Borneo to Beirut, then the inevitable Northern Ireland, throughout this book, I have tried to draw a picture of the experiences that many young soldiers endure in the pursuance of perfection.

Ultimately, what price perfection!